D1241411

The Man Who Called Himself Devlin

**Also by William M. Green**

See How They Run
The Salisbury Manuscript
Avery's Fortune
Spencer's Bag

# THE MAN WHO CALLED HIMSELF DEVLIN

## A Novel of Suspense
by
### William M. Green

FGC.1

**The Bobbs-Merrill Company, Inc.**
Indianapolis/New York

Copyright © 1978 by William M. Green

All rights reserved, including the right of reproduction
in whole or in part in any form
Published by The Bobbs-Merrill Company, Inc.
Indianapolis     New York

Designed by Rita Muncie
Manufactured in the United States of America

First printing

**Library of Congress Cataloging in Publication Data**

Green, William M., 1936-
  The man who called himself Devlin.

  I.  Title.
PZ4.G79814Man  [PS3557.R3757]  813'.5'4     78-55653
ISBN 0-672-52514-3

For Lindsay of the Waggeners

"In cities, mutinies; in countries, discord;
in palaces, treason . . . . ruinous disorders
follow us disquietly to our graves."

*King Lear*

The Man Who Called Himself Devlin

Times like these will give rise to men like Devlin.
You have read of the incident on Dhasai.
It has been called a massacre. It has been called
a rescue. It will depend on whose account you believe.
This is Devlin's account, set down in his own hand.

A. M. Hajab

blk o... ...u 634-0816

## 24 Personal Notices

### LINDA

Happy Anniversary
**LOVE RICH**

Happy ~~Birthday~~ to KAYCEE
Bes~~t~~ ~~~~ Birthday
...from

I can help you solve any problem. Worldwide. Absolute confidentiality. Min. fee 30,000. Contact Devlin. Box 150, Bridgetown, Barbados

sha... ...ther coupl Jun... ... Swimming, Skiing and outing.

**SOUTHSIDE PRESS**
24 HR. Service on business cards + Wedding invitations.

**WANT Marijuana legalized?**
Show support at Southeastway Park Sun June 11, 12 noon!

# 1

They said he had shown remorse, so they packed him off to the farm. Six months of manicured lawns, air-conditioned rooms, arts and crafts. He had never had it so good. But what else could they do with a fifteen-year-old who had wantonly taken a life? The law had been written for another world, a different time.

He had sat in the courtroom in a neat suit and tie, a slight young man, small boned and not quite five feet five inches tall, freshly scrubbed and carefully groomed, eyes downcast, lip atremble, on the edge of tears, a picture of abject remorse. Could an angel kill?

His mother had sat behind him, a wad of Kleenex in her hand, sponging up her tears. Madonna and child. A heartbreaking tableau.

The dead girl wasn't present, of course, to evoke pity; and her parents, biting back their grief, had only managed to look severe.

Whom would you have felt sorry for?

I got all this later, from the newspaper files, after the girl's parents made contact with me.

He had stepped out in front of her on the path in the park where she had been riding her bicycle. He wasn't wearing his suit and tie then. And slight in stature though he was, he was well muscled and wiry. He had stepped out suddenly from the shrubbery, and she had braked so as not to hit him. He had known she

3

would. Today's clever savage knows how to make capital of compassion. She had braked to avoid hitting him and had swerved and lost her balance. He had grabbed the bike and tried to pull it out from under her. She had clung to her property: simple reflex; she hadn't seen the sawed-off baseball bat in his hand. He had struck her repeatedly until she let go. It was a matter of public record.

The local fence would pay him fifteen dollars for the bike. The girl would die.

From the moment they caught him and throughout the booking procedure and the trial, he was the picture of remorse. He was not only a killer but a young man of extreme cunning. He did his six months on the juvenile farm and was set free.

I placed him under surveillance.

He came home like a hero, as if he'd just won the war. And maybe he had. He'd got away with murder. All the kids on the street turned out to lay their palms on his. They went off like firecrackers, all those slapping hands.

He spent part of the night with a girl in a burned-out Chevy in a rubble-strewn alley. He had the pick of them all. He was big medicine.

The next day he spent in harmless loitering, smoking rope with his peers, stripping the copper pipe from an abandoned building. Call it a recycling project. Perhaps he had truly benefited from his time on the farm. The state had given him six months. I had been instructed to give him three weeks. During that time it would be up to him to prove that indeed he had been rehabilitated. His future lay entirely in his hands. At eight o'clock in the morning, on the second day after his release, it began to slip away.

He had saved a foot-long piece of copper pipe from the building they had stripped. He slipped it under his shirt and carried it there, pressed between his side and his upper right arm. In his left hand he carried a big brassy transistor radio, a tubby noise box the size of a small valise. Thus appointed, he sauntered down Fifth Avenue southward from 110th Street. He entered the park just below the 96th Street transverse and found his way onto a wooded knoll above a footpath. He slipped the length of pipe out from under his shirt, set it down in the grass and sat down beside it, with his back against a tree. He adjusted the tuner and volume on his radio, tucked his knees up under his chin and waited, watching the occasional passerby.

There weren't many people to be seen so early on a weekday morning: occasional youngsters on their way to school on the other side of town, walking quickly in groups of two and three, dodging and dancing along the path, carefree as skylarks, carrying nothing of apparent value except their books.

The footpath curved toward him and away in a series of lazy S's, and he sat in the shadows at the base of one of the curves, so that he had a good view coming and going. I had an even better view, squatting in the shadow cast by a rock barely fifteen feet behind him. I remained absolutely still, as still as the rock that sheltered me.

He played his radio at extremely low volume, a barely audible thump and rumble, in order to avoid drawing attention to himself. The muted sound of reggae drifted up the hill to me, augmented by the occasional busy chatter of the schoolbound children and the cooing of courting pigeons. The city sounds, the sounds of traffic and horns beyond the trees on Fifth Avenue, seemed miles away.

I was up higher than he was, so I saw the old gentleman before he did, poking along the footpath, taking his time. He was dressed comfortably, in scuffed sandals and chino trousers. A frail avian figure in a shapeless gray sweater that covered a small pot belly and hung down around his hips. Around his neck he wore a pair of high-powered binoculars. A birdwatcher, on his way home. Even now, as he shambled down the path, slightly flatfooted, taking small, careful steps, his eyes were on the treetops. One more flash of color, rush of wing before breakfast. Oh! What a lovely autumn day.

The boy below me saw him coming with his old man's gait, saw the fine binoculars around his neck. He had an eye for value, that boy. His left hand faded down the volume on the radio and then turned it off. His right hand closed around the length of pipe. He crabbed backward a few feet so that the trunk of the tree shielded him from the path. There were no other persons in sight.

We could hear the old man's shoes scraping on the asphalt now. The boy studied the old man's progress passively, his back pressed against the tree. He would wait until his quarry had passed and then take him from behind.

As the old man rounded the little curve in the path

so that his back was to the wooded knoll, the boy moved silently into a crouch. I could see the muscles on his forearms tighten as his knuckles went white around the length of pipe. He began flexing his legs, bouncing lightly on his toes, preparing to spring. I moved first, so that as he uncoiled I was right behind him. The old birdwatcher sensed the stirring among the trees, turned and saw the boy break toward him, weapon raised. There could be no question as to his assailant's intent. One day the old man might have to bear witness to that fact.

The old man shied and tried to shield his head with his forearm. A futile gesture; the copper pipe would have snapped the frail arm as if it were kindling. Then he froze and gaped as the boy stopped cold in his tracks. My right hand caught his with its upraised weapon; my left forearm blocked his throat. He tried to throw me off. I drove my knee into the small of his back. For a moment I held the boy like that, using him as a shield to mask my identity while I shouted to the old man, "Run!"

He didn't run, exactly, but he scurried off at a brisk pace. I hoped he would notify the police. By the time he did, I would have finished what I had to do.

Small in stature as he was, the boy was strong. It was like trying to pin down a cobra. When he finally realized that he couldn't squirm out, he tried the psychological approach. Oh, they're masters at it, these little bastards. When all else fails, fall back on the whimpering importunation: "Please, man. You're hurting my back. Please, man. Have a heart." He sounded so pitiable I was almost moved to let him go.

You would have. It would have been your last act of kindness. He'd have thanked you for your humanity by laying his length of pipe across your skull.

I put my mouth close to his ear and whispered, "There'll be no parades when you come home this time. There'll be no more old men and little girls lying in the roadway. The wars are over for you, son."

He tried, with his free hand, to reach back and crush my genitals. I returned his affront in kind, ramming my knee up between his legs. He gasped and his body contracted violently. I let him drop. He lay curled up like a caterpillar among the fallen leaves. I picked up the length of pipe. I placed my hand over his mouth so that his cries would not bring people running. Then I used his weapon on his knees. He fainted with the first blow. He would live, but he wouldn't walk again. I propped him up against the tree he had used for cover and employed his weapon once more to break the first, second and third knuckles of each of his hands. Straight bones are easily repaired, joints hardly ever. Those hands would wield lethal weapons no more.

I unfolded the paper I had carried in my pocket and pinned it to his shirt as per instructions. Taped to the paper was a line scissored out of a book. "And justice shall be done." I recognized it as a line from Mackay's "Eternal Justice." The girl's parents had mailed it to me with my retainer. They would read about it in the papers in the morning. And they would know that, in their case at least, justice had been done.

Medieval? Perhaps. But there is something to be said for medieval punishment. It reduces the savages in the populace by each individual punished. It is not only foolhardy, it is uneconomic for a society to bankrupt itself in the rehabilitation of its undesirables. The world isn't short of people.

I tossed the kid's radio onto his lap and left the area. Since I saw no police heading for the park, I assumed that the old birdwatcher had simply hurried home to reflect on his good luck.

I stopped at a public telephone on Madison Avenue and advised the *Daily News* that, at a designated spot in the park, a story was developing that would be worth the attention of a photo-journalist. I knew that the boy would still be there when the *News* team arrived.

I took a cab to Rockefeller Center and rented a new P.O. box. Then I cabbed over to the *Times* and placed another ad in the Personals. Essentially it was the same as the ad I always used, except that the P.O. box was different.

> Any problem—worldwide. I can help you solve it. Absolute confidentiality. Min. fee 30,000. Mr. Devlin. Box 750, Radio City Station, New York

I used the public phone on the corner of Seventh Avenue and 44th Street to call the girl's parents and tell them the job had been done; they would find proof of it in tomorrow morning's paper. They expressed their gratitude and asked where to forward the fifteen thousand dollars still due me. I told them to save it and use it constructively. I must have been getting soft in the head. But I do have certain standards, and this assignment had demanded very little ingenuity and taken very little time.

I walked north through the soiled and sour-smelling morning-after streets of Times Square, past the tiresome, vacant-faced steel monoliths of the Fifties into the sunny arena of Columbus Circle at the southern edge of the park. I turned east and passed a flower shop, hesitated, and went in. I ordered a spray of roses delivered once a year on this date to the cemetery where the girl was buried. She would be forgotten all too soon.

It was a fine autumn day. Apple-crisp and clear. A splendid day to be alive. And you wonder what sort of monster could find delight in a day that had begun so brutally.

You think of the boy, maimed.

I think of the old man delivered from pain, and of the girl's parents, freed of remorse.

I think that I have done a service—for a price, it's true; a man must live. But you are the beneficiaries of my enterprise as surely as are the old man and the girl's parents. Because of what I did this morning, your nights will be that much less fraught with fear. Arrogant? Spare me the lecture. I know it by heart.

Allow a man to short-cut the law, and where will it end?

And where will it end if renegades like that boy have their way?

The law must serve as a shield for the innocent. But

who are the innocent? The old birdwatcher, or the boy?

And if the birdwatcher is one of the innocent, and if the boy is allowed to run free, then whom is the law protecting? Fear the boy, not me.

I may do what I do for money, unpleasant work that most men would shudder to contemplate. But I do what I do within the boundaries of what I sense to be right, within the realm of values established through the millennia by men striving to make life livable.

For a price I broke that boy. Do you imagine that I would have done the same, for any price, to the girl whom he brained for a bicycle?

Am I really so despicable? And aren't you really better off without that boy I set against the tree? And if the world has come to such a state that only men like me stand between men like you and the encroaching jungle, then who is to blame, and who has been delinquent in his stewardship of the world that was placed in his care?

# 2

I returned to the St. Regis and took the elevator up to my suite. Nor is it indiscreet of me so specifically to identify my quarters; they were only temporary, as was my identity. The management was totally unaware of the unsavory character of their guest, and by the time you read this I will have moved on a dozen times and employed a dozen different names.

The name I was born with is just a memory, recalled only dimly even by me. And all those, save one, to whom that name had meaning are gone—gone before their time, erased in the name of expediency, sold out to pander to a chimera! Self-determination. What folly! The old colonies simply changed masters; they hooked their umbilicals to new benefactors, the Soviets and the Americans, and called themselves free, much as fractious children cry independence while living off a dole from home.

I have seen the future according to the gospel of the catchphrases. I have lost my country and all I held dear. The fields my forebears tilled have been defiled. The sweet green land has turned to rot. And for what? Chaos and oppression such as no man had known under the orderly old regimes. Let them choke on their catchphrases.

I never went back, not even to decorate the graves. I joined the company of homeless men.

In my room, a whiskey and soda; a steaming bath. Life's little pleasures. Room service for a hearty brunch, an unlisted service for a good woman. Food and flesh. Life's rewards. I am a professional, and I deal with professionals in all things. I would no more scavenge for love than I would scavenge for dinner. Both my partner and I are thus enriched. One knows what one is getting. One gets what one pays for. No sweat, no frustration, no debts. No reprobation, please. I am the sort before whom innocence recoils. My features have been broken and pieced together so

12

often that my countenance, though reasonably pleasant to behold, is strangely devoid of expression: like a carefully fashioned plastic mask. And my flawlessly tailored clothing hides a body branded with scars.

As for the woman who comes to me for a fee, her body is hers to sell, to share, to give away, or to guard as zealously as a saint. She chooses to barter it, as I barter mine, as the athlete barters his. She is paid for her services, as I am paid for mine. And, make no mistake, my services encompass more than meting out punishment to recidivist boys.

I am a man without a country, a soldier without an army, a mercenary; the most recent incarnation of that long line of nomad warriors dating back to ancient Thrace, alternately despised and mythologized. We are an embarrassment even to those who hire us. But we are necessary.

On those moonless midnights when the barbarian lays siege to the gate—be he a little boy armed with an iron pipe, or a rocket-bearing gang of guerrillas—when duly authorized forces are shackled by statutes that were shaped to protect men of reason, who will hold the line?

I may not be the chap you would want to parade through high society, or take home for dinner. And God forbid I be introduced to your daughter. But were you on a lonely street, with footsteps moving up behind you and your heart pounding in your ears, you'd be damned glad to turn a corner and find me standing there. And I hope that, after I'd saved your neck, you'd not be so crass as to reprimand me for having dealt roughly with your assailant.

13

# 3

My young thug made the *Daily News* next day. A half-page photo on page one displayed him propped against the tree where I'd left him, with the note pinned to his lapel. The *Times* carried the story, too, without a photo, among the Metropolitan briefs, supplemented by an editorial warning the populace that there were monsters loose in the land. It took me a moment to realize that the monster they were referring to was not the boy but me.

By the second day my story had lost its sensation value and had been replaced by a cruising yacht overdue in the Indian Ocean.

I made the rounds of my P.O. boxes. In the first one I found a money order in the sum of $15,000, signed fictitiously, but from the parents of the girl. This, despite my releasing them from their obligation. And a note attached. "In Gratitude." In my Radio City box I found an engraved business card; its costly simplicity exuded wealth and power. John Heald. Petrolux. Lettered beneath in sepia ink—ink, not ball-point—in a firm, no-nonsense hand, a phone number and a single word: urgent.

I walked a quarter of a mile through the subterranean maze beneath Rockefeller Center until I found a bank of phone booths. The number I dialed apparently circumvented the main switchboard at Petrolux and rang Mr. Heald's office directly. An alert secretary put me through immediately, meaning that Mr. Heald did indeed consider our business urgent, so urgent that whatever other business he was doing at the moment was to be peremptorily interrupted in my favor.

"Heald."

"Devlin here."

"We're at Number One Battery Place. How soon can you be here?"

"Give me thirty minutes."

"Good. We'll talk then." Mr. Heald's voice was flat, midwestern American. Mr. Heald sounded unruffled and absolutely in command, whatever the urgency of our business.

I hailed a cab on Sixth Avenue, wedged myself into the narrow space behind the driver's plastic shield, and did my best to avoid suffering a crushed coccyx as the rattletrap machine bounced across 51st Street, found its way onto Broadway, and wove its way at breakneck speed down that crowded and pitted boulevard all the way to the southern tip of Manhattan. We arrived at Number One Battery Place intact and in twenty minutes' time. I paid the driver and allowed five minutes to elapse while watching a ferryboat maneuver into its slip. Then I entered the building.

Uniformed security men stood at the foot of each of three banks of elevators, checking identity cards. Those without cards were sent to a reception desk manned by more security people. The lunatic fringe had driven prudent men to paranoid extremes. There had been threats against Petrolux. Bombs had been left in the lobby. But that had been years ago. I doubted that that was why Mr. Heald had summoned me.

One of the guards at the elevator stood in my way and asked for my card. I told him I had none, but that I had an appointment with Mr. Heald. He had been alerted.

"Name, please, sir?"

"Devlin."

He stepped aside. "Yes, sir. The elevator to the forty-first floor, please."

I found myself alone in an express elevator. With ear-popping facility it sucked me up to the thirty-sixth floor. There it began a series of stops, accepting and disgorging an array of neatly turned out secretaries, custom-tailored executives, and assorted paper shufflers and messenger boys. I was alone again when we arrived at the forty-first floor. There was a receptionist to the right of the elevator bank and one to the left. A matching pair. Perhaps, in light of their stratospheric solitude, they were there to keep each other company. I faced right.

"Mr. Heald, please?"

"To your left."

I turned left and approached her twin.

"Mr. Heald?" I inquired.

"Mr. Devlin?"

I nodded.

"To your right."

She flashed a dentifrice model's smile and indicated the passageway behind her. There was a richly paneled solid wood door at the far end to the right. Glancing over my shoulder, I noticed another just like it at the extreme opposite end of the passageway. With geometrically arranged receptionists at either end of the elevator bank and with geometrically arranged doors at either end of my passageway, there must be twin doors at either end of the opposite passageway, which meant that the entire forty-first floor was divided into just four suites of offices. I was not only high up in the superstructure: I was very near the top in the corporate structure.

I was also in a virtual trap. If this meeting was bait, someone had only to pull the string to net me. One armed man set neatly down between the matching pair of receptionists could cut me off from the elevator. I wondered where the fire stairs were. I don't like towers at all.

The doorknob was gold plated and as large as a ship's wheel. There was no name on the door, no buzzer, no knocker. It would have been folly to rap with one's knuckles on so formidable a barrier, so I reached out to rotate the knob. It turned with fluid ease before I could touch it, and the door swung slowly away from me, as if the whole thing operated on gears within gears within gears; all copiously lubricated, no doubt, with Petrolux Oil.

A sunny reception room greeted me, and an equally sunny receptionist.

"Mr. Devlin?" One of her sisters near the elevator must have alerted her while I was making my way down the corridor. "Would you follow me, please? Mr. Heald is expecting you."

That would be the understatement of the day; I'd been through more checks than a larcenous paymaster.

She led me past a series of small, well-appointed offices, each about the size of a first-class railroad compartment, manned by busy secretaries; I counted four, and two conference rooms—at the moment unoccupied—and floor-to-ceiling glass all the way.

At last, in a loungelike area, I was introduced to a tall, handsome woman dressed in costly blue velour who was Heald's most private and personal aide. She reassured me that I was expected and invited me to follow her, without delay, into Mr. Heald's private office. She tapped peremptorily on his door and, without waiting for a reply, went in.

Mr. Heald, squat and well tailored, turned from the window, where, I assumed, he had been doing some hard creative thinking, or maybe just enjoying the spectacular view. Pink faced, fortyish, he moved briskly across the opulent cream-colored carpet on Gucci shoes, hand extended. For all his cherub look, he was no innocent. Sharp blue eyes behind aviator eyeglasses were doing a thorough job sizing me up.

"Right on schedule, Mr. Devlin."

"I try to be."

"Something to drink?"

"No, thank you."

"Have a seat."

There were lounge chairs set about an immense marble-topped coffee table. There was no desk in evidence anywhere. An office without a desk: a conceit of certain members of the executive class. Some manila folders lay on the coffee table, and a speaker box to amplify phone calls, and a clipboard with a blank sheet of paper in it. There was a sideboard against the left wall, its surface arranged with neat stacks of folders and papers. The back wall was lined with technical books. Ponderous volumes bound in somber colors. There was a large, stark Motherwell on the right-hand wall, and a closed door which, if my past experience in executive suites applied, gave onto a private bathroom. The walls were citrus-yellow. The furled curtains were transparent and diaphanous. The lady in velour had departed silently, and silently closed the door behind her. I could have faced the painting or the window. I eschewed both stunning views in favor of a chair that faced the door. Caution before aesthetic delights.

Heald sat down across from me, leaned over, pressed a button on the talk box, and asked for no interruptions. He opened one of the manila folders and began leafing through the pages inside, glancing up at me intermittently. From where I sat, the pages looked like make sheets, the kind you see in post offices, with front and profile pictures at the top and half a page of type underneath.

At one point he stopped turning over the pages, looked up at me, then down again at the 8½x11 sheet, then up at me again. "Looks good to me, Mr. . . . ah . . . Devlin?"

"Devlin."

He smiled puckishly, lifted the sheet out of its folder and sailed it to me across the table. "Does that look about right to you?"

There was my mug shot, passport size, full face and profile, poignantly youthful: a copy of an ID set taken long ago in a more careless time. It belonged to another incarnation and bore only a vague resemblance to my present appearance. It was as if I had been presented with pictures (evidence) of an estranged son. Among the aliases was my real name, which must have been what he was smiling about. And that was distressing. In my mind armed men materialized at the elevator door. There were newspaper clippings of a number of my more recent adventures. Also a tightly printed résumé of my background and experience, disturbingly correct, dating back to the Grenadier Guards, a callow nineteen, special commando training, special operations, citations, civilian life. Sheep ranch, marriage, everything. Loss of everything. Soldier for hire. There was even a thumbprint.

"I thought I'd covered my tracks." I affected nonchalance, but I felt decidedly uneasy.

"We have the world's best trackers. We have the world's best—period. We can afford it."

"I hope you can afford me."

"Depends on your price."

"Depends on your job."

"If we want you, we'll afford you." Sparring. To what end?

He went to the sideboard and came back with a small ink pad and a sheet of blank paper. "To verify the thumbprint; I hope you don't mind. There is a vague facial resemblance to the photos, but we like to be sure."

"I do mind. I don't like anyone to be that sure about me. You'll take me at face value or not at all."

"I think we'll take you, Mr. . . . ah . . ." A regular tease, that one.

"Devlin."

"Of course." Of course they'd block the fire stairs, too.

"I don't suppose the whole book there is devoted to me?"

"Not at all. There are eleven others. Not all available at the moment. Not all in good health." I studied him for telltale signs of apprehension. None.

"It's not at all a salubrious profession."

"I wouldn't think so. I wouldn't be in it for the world."

"Most men wouldn't be. That's why you rely on us."

"I suppose it has its rewards, judging from the rate quoted in your advertisement."

"Disabuse yourself of the idea of any bargains. The rate quoted is my minimum fee. And I'll want that dossier before I leave." If they were coming for me, they would have been at the door by now. I let my arm dangle; there was a pistol in the holster strapped to my calf.

"I appreciate that. If we were bargain hunting, Mr. Devlin, we wouldn't have contacted you. Remember, we hire only the best. I'll tell you what our problem is, and you tell me if you can handle it. Then we'll fix a price."

I nodded my assent. In my mind's eye the gunmen at the exits began to withdraw, lose substance, evaporate into the air from which they had materialized. I began to feel at ease. This is the way we live . . . or die.

"You ever heard of Dhasai?"

I had to think a moment. Then I placed it. "An island, isn't it? In the Persian Gulf."

Heald looked surprised. "I wouldn't have thought you'd know it. It's not much more than a flyspeck on the water."

"I know the territory."

"Of course. It's on your sheet. What else do you know about the island?"

"Not much. It's a supply depot of some kind. No one really lives there."

"No one really lives there except the crews that man it, and they're only there for thirty days at a time, on rotation." As he talked he was scratching away at a note pad with a Mont Blanc pen as fat as a sausage. "Roughly, that's it." He tore off the sheet of paper and passed it to me across the marble tabletop.

It was a very sketchily drawn map of an area of the Persian Gulf.

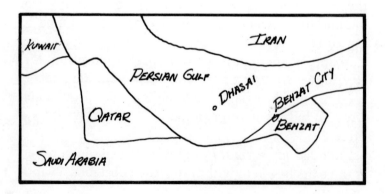

"It's not exactly a supply depot."

"What is it," I asked, "—a drilling site?"

"No. A distribution center. All the platforms in that quarter of the Gulf pump their product by submarine pipeline into Dhasai. Those are Petrolux platforms operating under a complicated pattern of leasing agreements with the sheikdom of Behzat. Dhasai is also run by us under lease from Behzat. Petrolux is all there is on Dhasai. Storage tanks, pipeline terminals, docks for our tankers. The oil is pumped in there. The tankers tie up, fill up, pull out. The place isn't good for anything else. No wildlife, no vegetation, no soil to speak of. Just coral, sand and pumice. But it's one of the most valuable pieces of real estate in God's creation. Everything pumped out of that part of the Gulf goes through there; a couple of million dollars' worth of crude a day. What's more, the pumps on all our wells in that area are controlled from a master station on the island. Just like a kitchen with a mess of faucets, and you can tap any damn reservoir you want."

"Very neat."

"Yeah. A masterpiece of modern engineering." He had opened his coat and begun gently to knead his belly. "The guy who designed the system is a genius. Made his pile, and now he's to hell and gone, dreaming up some other fancy thing. That's the advantage of being creative over being administrative. You can always move on to something else."

Heald had begun to look positively bilious. He stabbed a button on his phone box and called, "Janice. Maalox, please." He looked at me inquiringly. "You don't want some, do you?" and answered his own question: "Of course not. You're the kind can always move on."

There came a brisk tapping at the door.

"O.K., Janice," Heald bellowed. And then, to me: " *1aalox before lunch. That's what the top floor will get you." He burped loudly and made a sour face as the blue velour lady entered with a tray. She seemed prepared to stand by and spoon-feed him, but he dismissed her. "Thanks, hon. Just leave it." She bent gracefully at the knee, like an airline stewardess, set the tray down on the table, and left without a word.

Heald spooned out a dose of Maalox, licked the residue off his lips, belched again and asked, "Now, where were we?" He looked all pink and freshly scrubbed again.

"On Dhasai. Turning on the faucets."

"Yeah. Well, that's exactly the trouble. The faucets are all turned on. The oil is flowing in, but it's got no outlet. Our best estimate is that in four more days the storage tanks on the island will be full to bursting. Five more days and they'll rupture. Damned island will be awash in oil. Pretty blue Gulf will turn black with it."

"Why don't you turn off your faucets?"

"Can't do that."

"You've got a backup system on the individual platforms. Turn it off at the source."

"We're trying. A waste of money. A waste of time. Given the manpower available and the number of rigs in the Gulf, it will take a couple of weeks to shut down that whole field."

"Too late."

24

"You don't know the half of it. Even if we could shut down all those rigs tomorrow, there's enough crude already in the pipelines between the platforms and Dhasai to rupture the holding tanks. As long as those pumps on Dhasai keep sucking it up, we're dead ducks."

There was a piece missing here. Something he wasn't telling me; either deliberately withheld or withheld because it was so clear and present in his mind that he assumed it to be understood.

"Where are your tankers?" I asked. "Why don't you bring in every tanker within range? Keep filling them up until the crisis is over?"

"Can't do that either. We just got through rerouting all our tankers away from the place, all except the one that was there already. Can't let 'em near there, and can't tell 'em why."

"I'd say you've got trouble."

"You bet your sweet ass." He leaned toward me across that great plateau of a coffee table in an attitude of confidentiality and fixed me with his delft-blue eyes. "Let me tell you something about engineering marvels, like our control station on Dhasai. They are two-headed monsters. They make it possible for a handful of men to control the day-to-day function of a huge enterprise. By the same token"—he made a fist of his pudgy right hand; his knuckles went white—"it takes only a handful of men"—his baby-pink face went lavender—"to fuck it all up completely."

I waited until his normal color returned. "You want me to go to Dhasai and . . . turn off your faucets?"

He nodded and poured himself another shot of Maalox. "But it's not that easy."

"I didn't think it would be; otherwise you wouldn't have contacted me. The island is occupied, isn't it?"

His clear blue eyes went wide. "How the hell did you know that?" In his voice, for the first time, were intimations of the meanness that had gotten this pudgy cherub to the forty-first floor.

"Why else couldn't you turn off your faucets?"

"Jesus! If you knew what lengths we've gone to to keep it quiet. Just a handful of us here at Petrolux. Our tanker captains don't even know why they were re-routed. But we can't keep the lid on forever. For one thing, the oil will be spilling off the island into the Gulf in less than a week. But I told you that already, didn't I? Jesus! Do you know exactly how many millions that represents?"

"What about your men on the island? Or did they get off?"

"Get off? How in the world could they get off? They're stuck there, along with the crew of the one tanker that was tied up at the dock when the shit hit the fan."

"How many are there?"

"Maybe four or five hundred in all."

"You know exactly how much money you're losing each day, but only approximately how many men you've trapped there?"

"My end of the business is money. Somebody else takes care of the personnel. I'll tell you this, though. They get rotated every thirty days. That's just three or four days from now. So, about the same time the oil starts flooding the Gulf, those men's families are going to wonder why they aren't home for their monthly rotation. Any way you look at it, we can't keep the lid on much longer."

"When did the occupation begin?"

"Three days ago."

"Why hasn't the word got out?"

"Because communication to the mainland is by telephone. We control the switchboard in Behzat City. We decided if we could keep the lid on, we could keep down hysteria. We didn't want the kind of pressure that can cave you in."

"What else have you done?"

"We've made a pass at negotiating with them."

"You've sent a man there?"

"Over the phone. They'll allow no one on the island. You can't send a plane or boat in; they're afraid of what else might be on it."

"Progress?"

"None. There can't be. I don't want to think about the day they realize that negotiation is out of the question."

"Why?"

"You think we should deal with them?" He looked astonished.

"No. But half the world seems to try. Why not you?"

"We aren't in a position to. We lease from the government of Behzat. The government of Behzat is the one that's clamped the lid on."

I looked skeptical. "Who controls Behzat?"

Heald looked wary. "Behzat is a sovereign state."

"Until five or six years ago, Behzat was nothing but a mess of tents and sand."

"Well, head for head, it's now the richest little piece of real estate in the world."

"And who's responsible for that?"

"Ask the sheik. He's the ruler. And a darned enlightened one, all things considered."

"The sheik just stepped out of the tenth century. He's still trying to adjust to the light. Who rules the sheik?"

Heald looked annoyed and then just shrugged. "Who rules the world?"

We both knew the answer to that one. Oil. And someone was trying to keep it from its rightful owners.

"So who's clamped the lid on? Petrolux or Behzat?"

"Does it matter?"

"I like to know whom I'm working for."

"You're working for Petrolux."

"Whom am I working against?"

He didn't pause for effect; he didn't have to. "Armageddon."

I found that puzzling. Armageddon was a West German gang: urban guerrillas with a taste for grandiloquent names.

"In the Middle East?" I asked incredulously.

Heald nodded grimly.

"They're European."

"They're going global," Heald stated flatly.

"They're not doing all that well at home."

"Maybe that's why they're going abroad. Kind of marketing and development consultants in the manufacture of revolution. They've got leadership. You've got dissidents. They'll help you articulate your grievances."

"Anyplace?"

"Anyplace they consider pivotal to a general collapse of order. Someone creates a crisis in the Persian Gulf, I'd say he's getting pretty pivotal."

"So in the end it comes down to who rules the world—Petrolux or Armageddon?"

"Maybe. Which would you choose?"

"I've already had a taste of armageddon."


Heald filled me in as best he could on the situation on the island. Nobody knew an awful lot. The only communication had been by phone with the man who spoke for the invaders. He spoke French, but it was heavily accented with German. He called himself Woden. Why not? A god.

Petrolux had no idea how many men were in the occupation force, but they assumed it had to be substantial in order to hold four or five hundred men in submission. I disagreed. Properly armed, they could do it with a couple of dozen men. With half a dozen. Unarmed, without discipline or leadership, the captives, however many, were a headless body; a mob. The invaders, however few, were an army, motivated by their grievance against Behzat or Petrolux or both, disciplined by Woden. You can't beat an army with a mob. You must have a better army.


I got out of the chair and stretched my legs and took in the view of the bay. Then I turned back to Heald.

"Take away Armageddon for the moment. Take away Woden. Who are these people on Dhasai?"

"The terrorists?"

"Let's not call them terrorists. It's a word that serves them, not us. It promotes hysteria. It makes them seem more formidable than they are."

"They're mostly Bahwabi Muslims. They speak for a hefty minority of the population of Behzat; at least they claim they do. Who knows who really speaks for whom nowadays? A few years ago some of them occupied a bank, took hostages, were cornered, issued demands, surrendered and were locked up. I think about half a dozen of them were involved. A year or so later their disciples took more hostages to free the original members of their group. A few people on either side were hurt that time out, and another half-dozen were taken into custody. The incidents began to multiply, one feeding on the other. By now there may be thirty or forty of the terrorists . . ."

"Extremists."

". . . extremists in jail. And maybe half that number of innocent civilians have been hurt or killed. So it's grown steadily worse with time, but it really had no direction, no cohesion, until just recently, when Armageddon moved in."

"What's their beef?"

"Armageddon?"

"We know what Armageddon wants. Chaos. Anywhere. The Bahwabis."

"Return to the homeland."

"Where's their homeland?"

"It doesn't exist anymore. Hasn't for over fifty years.

Vanished with the dissolution of the Ottoman Empire after World War I. It's now part of three different sheikdoms south and west of Behzat."

"Behzat won't let them emigrate?"

"Behzat would like nothing better. They *can't* emigrate. The other sheikdoms won't have them. The Bahwabis want Bahzat to mount a campaign to take back their homeland for them. If the present regime won't agree to this adventure, they'll do their damndest to topple it and replace it with one that will. Madness!"

"The state of the world."

"I fail to understand it."

How could he? He had never lost anything.

He turned ruminative. "Time was an émigré was grateful for his new homeland. Embraced it. Became one with it. God knows the old country couldn't have been all that kind to him, or he'd never have left it in the first place." I could only smile at his certitude. He had never been an exile.

He expanded. "That's the way it was in my grandfather's time. What was wrong with that? Now everyone's gone native. The cult of the ethnics. Running around resurrecting all those mouldy memories their grandparents did their damndest to forget."

He was right in his way. Nobody knew better than I the futility of trying to disinter the past. You cannot call back yesterday. You cannot drape yourself in the moth-eaten bunting of nations turned to dust.

"A reversion to tribalism," Heald muttered. "Who's leading them on? The Commies?"

"The chiefs."

He looked at me quizzically. "What chiefs?"

"The unemployed chiefs. Every tribe needs a chief. The more tribes, the more chiefs. Nice work for the chiefs. Diminishing returns for the members of the tribe. They mortgage their kids' future for the sake of a little coziness now. They hang them up in limbo somewhere between what is and what used to be. The old land is gone and they won't accept the new. Outsiders forever."

"Damn world's getting like a sprung clock. There are so many loose pieces, nobody'll ever be able to make it run again." Heald successfully managed a belch. "Look at what we've got in Behzat. If the standing government gives in to these fanatics, they lose the support of a substantial portion of the population. If the government fights them, they lose another, smaller but still substantial, part of the population. They are, my friend, caught by the short hairs. If we can keep this situation on Dhasai quiet, things may return to normal. If passions are aroused, the regime in Behzat City may fall; leftist elements may take over . . ."

"And you may lose not only your leases but your capital investment."

"In the Gulf. Right. But that's only the tip of the iceberg. We could lose it worldwide. Pipelines, rigs, tankers, refineries—they're all easy marks. Big as we are, we could go down like the *Titanic*."

"You understand the risk you're taking by hanging tough?"

"Every time we drill a hole, we take a risk."

"This is a different kind of risk. There are four or

five hundred men on that island. Maybe women and children."

"Thank God, no women or children."

"O.K. The women and children are at home. And those men are their husbands, fathers, sons, brothers." He got my meaning, but his resolve didn't waver. Why should it? He wasn't on the island.

He leaned forward and fixed me with another look of confidentiality from across the great plateau of marble. "Let me explain something to you. The Bahwabis' quarrel isn't with us—it's with Behzat; we're just a handy lever. We can't afford to let ourselves be that handy. Once the word gets out that we can be had, we'll be the target of every crackpot with a grievance from here to Timbuktu. Let 'em start nicking a vein here, nicking a vein there, nicking a vein any damn where they choose, and before you know it we've been bled prostrate. So we hang tough."

"And if more than an acceptable number of lives is lost, or if that crude spills out into the Gulf and causes an ecological disaster . . . ?"

"We take that risk. God, how I envy the Germans and the Jews. They pulled off their rescues so nice and clean. They were the world's darlings . . ."

"Yeah. But think of what the world would have had to say if they'd failed."

He swallowed hard, and his complexion took on that bilious color again.

# 4

Before I left Mr. Heald's office, Janice—I never did learn her last name—had booked me onto the Concorde to Paris and a connecting flight to Behzat City. Same time next morning I was overflying Dhasai in the observer's seat of a Behzatian Air Force reconnaissance jet. We made our first pass in a northwesterly direction at an altitude of 32,000 feet across the Persian Gulf from Behzat to Kuwait and kept going until we were over the horizon. We spent about twenty minutes circling around to the west and then made another run across the island from Qatar to Iran, this time at thirty-six thousand feet and on a direct line from west to east. The idea was to avoid looking like what we were, which was a Behzatian Air Force reconnaissance jet shooting three frames a second of 35 mm film as we crossed the island. All we got was about twenty-five frames on each pass, because the island of Dhasai, rising like a gray wart on the teal-blue surface of the sea, was barely more than a mile square.

We crossed the horizon again. This time when we came back we followed a course well to the south and out of sight of the island. We landed at Behzat City, and I rushed the films to the lab.

Fifteen minutes later the first blowups began coming out of the tank, still damp and reeking of developing fluid.

The pictures, magnified enormously, brought into unsettling focus a leprous landscape, lava-gray like the moon, with a cracked, parched surface laced with ropey pipelines like varicose veins. Bright blue-orange flames erupted at various junctures in the system, burning off the sour gas that bubbled through the pipelines. Tendrils of soupy brown smoke, like the effluence of bursting postules, smeared the hellish scene. The island looked like a battlefield, though no battle had taken place there. I was informed by the company man who went over the pictures with me that this was the everyday look of the place. Four long barrackslike buildings in the southeast corner of the island formed a quadrangle and normally provided sleeping and eating facilities for the workers, now prisoners. Three of the big buildings were dormitories; the fourth was a dining hall. Set apart from the barracks was a tiny community of cottages, five in all, where the foremen and managers lived. Question: Did they still reside in the cottages under guard, or had they been removed to the barracks? Question: Were all the barracks lived in now, as they had been before the island was occupied, or had everyone been herded into one building?

It could be determined from the photos that the prisoners were allowed a little mobility. At the time of our second pass over the island, there were several dozen figures scattered randomly about the quadrangle. One appeared to be sleeping at the base of one of the buildings. The question remained as to whether this was a specified exercise period at a specified time, or whether the prisoners had the freedom of the quadrangle at almost any time. Further reconnaissance flights could help us to make a judgment, but there was no time for protracted reconnaissance, nor did we wish to risk making the occupiers aware that they were being observed.

It was evident from the photographs that the quadrangle was under guard. Two figures could be seen on the rooftops of two of the barracks: certainly not prisoners and certainly armed. Type of weapons, unknown. But if they ran true to form, they would be carrying Soviet AK-47s and grenades.

Four men guarding the quadrangle during the day. One would have to assume that there were at least four more in the group to spell the daytime shift. Of course, if all the captives were packed into one barracks at night, just a couple of guards properly equipped could do the job. So maybe there were just ten invaders in all. It would be more prudent, though, to assume that there were at least sixteen, maybe more. That would be one of the first things about which I would have to make a determination after landing on the island.

As far as the island itself was concerned, we were dealing with a barren scrap of land, irregularly circular in shape and a little more than a mile square in total area. High ground, starting with a cliff of moderate altitude in the northeastern quarter, sloped down to sea level in the south. An escalloped shoreline running around from the south and up the western side of the island led to the piers. There were berths for eight tankers. One of the berths was filled, but the ship wasn't loading, nor was there anyone on any of her decks. She had a dead and abandoned look. It would have to be assumed that her crew was dead, or had been taken off and installed in the barracks. For the intruders to have left the crew on the ship where they would have to be guarded would have spread their forces too thin.

Three huge squat structures under construction in the waterfront area would house refrigerator plants that would transform excess gas, the gas that was now being flared off, into liquid at minus 265 degrees Fahrenheit. It could then be pumped into special tankers engineered like thermos bottles to keep the gas in a liquid state until it reached its destination. Ranked behind the construction site were the vast oil storage tanks and the control station, a large, squat structure that housed Mr. Heald's "faucets." Actually, it was the computer-controlled nerve center of the island, a facility requiring the operating skill of highly trained technicians. A rather unprepossessing structure, considering that it regulated all the oil-producing activity within a sixty-mile radius in the Persian Gulf, the total wealth of the sheikdom of Behzat, the black ink in the bookkeeper's pens at mighty Petrolux.

Dozens of offshore rigs pumped a half-million barrels a day through a network of submarine pipes to the island of Dhasai. Dhasai, in turn, like a bloated sow, fed the fleets of ships that came to suck at her western piers.

Toward the center of the island, behind the bungalows, a baseball diamond was laid out, of crushed coral; there were three tennis courts, of crushed coral; a nine-hole golf course, rat-gray like the rest of the island, with coral fairways and "greens" of oiled sand. They were greens in name only, for there was no green anywhere on the island. The soccer field was of oiled sand. It was as if men had colonized the moon and had done their best with the materials at hand to make it look like home. On the western shore, north of the piers, four small sailboats were tied up to buoys in a cove.

A few hundred yards from the island, off the northeast coast, was a patch of coral perhaps thirty feet long and ten feet wide. And some miles beyond that, stretching to the distant shore, the glistening sea was strewn with drilling rigs, the sun striking off steel platforms as precious as gems.

# 5

I packed up my pictures, left the briefing room, and dashed across the blistering tarmac to the air-conditioned car that had been put at my disposal. I left the air base and took the seaside road to the offices of the minister of the interior. There wasn't a lot of interior to administer in Behzat, but there was a hell of a lot just offshore, and that's what Minister Hajab was really in charge of. The seaside road wasn't the most direct route to Hajab's offices, but it was the least congested, and I had been advised not to risk an engine boilover in one of the more depressed neighborhoods of the city. Nor was the shore road exactly a scenic route. The harbor looked like the site of a traffic accident on a busy street corner. Scores of freighters jumbled together every which way, waiting for a place at the piers from which to unload, and beyond them, stretching out to sea, more freighters, queued up, waiting. Some of them, I had been told, had been waiting for months. The little sheikdom's sudden affluence had made possible an incredible influx of goods and materials, but no provision had been made for storage or orderly distribution. On the docks and spilling over onto the very fringes of the highway, mountains of flour sacks, in some places three or four stories high, split, crawling with rats, leaking, their precious burden soaking up humidity and sun, turning to paste. Sacks of concrete for construction turning to stone. Piles of such stone rivaling the pyramids. The intent was to share some of the wealth, but the organization wasn't there yet, and in a way it was worse than if there had been no flour at all. And beyond the infested sacks of flour, hundreds of automobiles, the best from Europe and America, parked bumper to bumper on the docks where they had been offloaded, their colors fading in the sun, their protective envelopes of grease turning rancid in the blowtorch air. And, shuttling back and forth between the lines of ships and the shore, giant Sikorsky helicopters swinging baggage nets beneath their bellies, working overtime to move matériel from the freighters' holds and, through their efforts, adding to the festering mess dockside. And the city itself, a jumble of hovels and gleaming high rises, a fetid patchwork of opulence and squalor. Behzat might solve its problems with the help of Petrolux and time. But was there time?

Hajab's office was deliciously cool.

His clothes were impeccably tailored and salad-crisp. He led me to a comfortable chrome and leather chair on one side of a Lucite desk, crossed around and sat down in a matching chair, except that his chair swiveled and rocked, as befitted an official of the wealthiest per capita state on the face of the earth. A little time out for some civilized prologue before getting down to business: he inquired about my car, my accommodations, and my impressions of his country.

I told him that my car ran splendidly; I had not yet had an opportunity to examine my accommodations and that his sheik's good intentions, as far as his people's welfare was concerned, were being woefully stymied by the impossible congestion in the port. He needed a good harbormaster.

He sighed. "You must realize that we are new to all this. Our administrative and line personnel are limited. What with the management of our resources on the one hand and our extremists on the other, the clearing of the docks is low on the list of priorities."

"May I respectfully suggest that there might be less support for the extremists if the more essential goods on the docks were distributed? Perhaps Petrolux could help."

"The sheik will not hear of it. Petrolux is already too much in control of our destiny."

"You allowed them to bring me in."

"The problem on Dhasai relates to our mineral wealth. Over that, Petrolux has jurisdiction. Which brings us to the matter at hand."

I nodded and brought out the pad I'd begun jotting notes on after the last pass over the island. I read to Hajab from the notes.

"Problem: To make a landing on the island unobserved, remain under cover long enough to reconnoiter, assess the situation at first hand, and then mount a coordinated assault on a number of strong points still to be determined.

"Problem: To land a force of fighting men on the island with enough surprise to knock out the invaders with minimal civilian casualties (it would be less than realistic to hope for zero casualties)."

Hajab nodded soberly. "I have one more problem to add to those already outlined. Time."

"I'm aware of the overflow problem with the oil."

"That would be approximately four days away. We have even less time than that."

"Then I have been misinformed. Explain, please."

"We have been in 'negotiation' with these bandits for nearly three days. It has by now become apparent to them that we are not negotiating but delaying. We were notified last night by telephone from the island that, in their generosity, the first three days of their occupation of the island were free. In order to stimulate our cooperation, there would begin, with this morning, a penalty for each day the situation went unresolved. One prisoner will be selected at random each morning and will be shot." He glanced at his watch. "The first prisoner will have been shot at six o'clock this morning."

That accounted for the "sleeping figure" in one of the blowups of the quadrangle. I offered the only recommendation I could in the appalling circumstance. "You have an army. Launch an assault."

"It would cost lives."

"Each day's delay will cost lives. How many days can you afford to delay before the casualties of delay surpass what you would lose in an assault?"

"What sort of assault would you mount in this situation? An amphibious landing?"

"Certainly not. They could see a force coming miles away. By the time your men hit the beaches, every prisoner on the island might have been slaughtered."

"An amphibious landing would be out of the question in any event. We have an army trained and equipped for the defense of our borders, and those are in the desert. Is there a feasible way of assaulting an island such as this?"

"An air drop. Perhaps a hundred parachutists in one quick overfly of the island. The surprise element is essential."

"There would be no casualties this way?"

"Of course there would be casualties. But I would guess that most of them would be soldiers, not civilians, and that there would be fewer of them than if you continued your 'negotiation' for a week."

"How long would it take for you to raise a force of parachutists?"

"I take that to mean that you have no parachute troops?"

"As I told you, our forces are defensive. We are a small country. Whom would we attack with parachute troops? So, I repeat: How long would it take you to raise such a force?"

"Too long. I could round up perhaps a dozen in a week's time. But we don't have a week, and a dozen men are not enough for this kind of assault. It would take weeks more to train a force of the required size."

"Impossible."

"I might drop a handful of men in from the sky and pin down this Woden long enough to give your regular armed forces time to make a landing. Surely you have gunboats. You could bring them in on gunboats and land them from inflatables."

"Again impossible. The truth is, we cannot use any troops of our government. These pirates claim to speak for a certain restless segment of our population; in truth they speak only for themselves. Whatever. We cannot make an overt move against them without the serious risk of precipitating a civil war. That is why you have been brought in."

"You're making an overt move by employing me."

"I must make it clear that we are not employing you."

"Petrolux, then."

"Petrolux neither. Those same internal and external political considerations that make it impossible for us to act must neutralize Petrolux also. We are so linked to Petrolux that if Petrolux employs you, it is practically the same as if we employ you. I must make it clear that, should anything go wrong, you will be honor bound to protect us. You may say no more than that you were acting in behalf of anonymous 'friends' of certain prisoners."

"The truth is you aren't all that concerned about the prisoners, are you? Your prime concern is the oil."

"Perhaps. But the prisoners will benefit, nonetheless. What's the difference where our motives lie? Now, can you tell me how long it will take you to recruit a suitable force?"

"In the circumstances, too long."

Hajab looked dismayed. "Am I to understand you are refusing the commission? Perhaps in light of the desperate nature of the situation, you consider your fee inadequate?"

"The fee is ample. The time is inadequate."

"We can offer you the best communications facilities to contact the personnel you need. We can place our air force at your disposal to fly them here— anonymously, of course—if transportation should be a problem. You have four days before the storage tanks begin to fail. In truth, you probably have close to a week. We may have underestimated the resilience and the capacity of the tanks in the interest of expediting the mission."

"Minister, they have begun to shoot a hostage a day. In seven days, seven men."

He looked chastened, and then, suddenly, hopeful. "Then you are not refusing the commission."

"I am not."

44

"And you will raise a fighting force."

"I cannot. Not the kind of force I need. I doubt that there are a hundred unaligned parachute troops available. I could round up a few men and use them to help me train a few dozen more. It would take weeks longer than even your most liberal estimate of the storage tanks' capacity. Certainly longer than the prisoners could afford to wait, wondering each morning which of them would buy it. How do you suppose he picks his candidates? At random? Alphabetically? According to height, weight, color? Russian roulette, day after day. Do you think you could survive that?"

"What do you suggest then?"

"The only alternative available: that we build our force from among the prisoners themselves."

# 6

Hajab threw me a despairing look. "You said it would take weeks to train a strike force of soldiers. Certainly it will take longer to train civilians. We have agreed that we don't have weeks to spare. Mr. Devlin, I cannot envision how you would drill your prisoner volunteers in the quadrangle while their captors complacently stand by and watch. Please, spare me this, Mr. Devlin."

"If you find my proposal unsatisfactory, void our contract."

"In favor of what? We have spent every waking moment in search of an unaligned commander."

"Then?"

He slumped in his seat, deflated, at a loss. "What are we to do, Mr. Devlin? There is no way we can win. If we accede to their demands, we have lost. If we mount an assault with our own troops, we have lost and, because it will be a slow-moving, seaborne assault, the lives of the hostages will be lost as well."

The poor bastard looked so distraught I decided I'd better take him by the hand and lead him back the way we'd come. "Let me break it down for you. A massive parachute drop would be the quickest, surest, safest way of recapturing Dhasai. Parachutists are specialists. To train a man, physically and tactically, to take part in such a specialized maneuver takes time. We don't have time. The foot soldier is another story. To be sure, he is a specialist, too, but of a far more common sort than the parachutist. We live in a world that has been at war in one way or another almost constantly for some thirty-five years. I'd be willing to bet that a fair percentage of the male prisoners on the island have had their share of basic military training. I would bet that a smaller percentage—but enough to help me do the job I have in mind—have had combat experience, under fire. In all probability, a select few of those are more experienced fighting men than most of the bandits holding them prisoner. I'll stake my life on it. There are, then, three things that must be done if we are to break the occupation of Dhasai. First, I must know who these few men are who can help. I need to know their names and what they look like. Second, I must gain access to the island, unobserved. Third, I must find those men among the prisoners, make my mission known to them, and see to it that they will be willing to go to some risk to help me. If I've chosen well, they will."

Hajab looked desolate. "I don't know how, in the few days we have, you can accomplish the first of your tasks, much less the second and third."

"Minister, with your cooperation, I guarantee you, I can accomplish the first of those objectives before lunch. The second objective will take a little longer and entail considerably more risk. As for the rest of it, I wouldn't venture odds. But I'll tell you this: I'll have those prisoners out of there in four days' time, or I'll be dead."

# 7

The regional offices of Petrolux were in their own spanking-new high rise a short way down a bone-white boulevard. I asked the minister to leave word where he might be reached should he have to leave his office. Then I took the elevator down and walked the two blocks to Petrolux. The streets were oven-hot, and I loved it. Some men are Eskimos; some are salamanders. The heat that weakened and depressed so many merely oiled up my joints and helped my muscles flex. I went through the standard Petrolux security checks and was directed to the department of personnel. Hajab had called ahead, and an efficient clerk was in the process of pulling the dossiers on all Petrolux employees currently on duty on Dhasai. The clerk was ignorant of the situation on the island, as were all but a handful of top Petrolux management. He had been told by his superior what his superior had been told by Hajab: I was a stateside coordinator scouting staff for a new feeder station to be modeled after Dhasai.

I was given a private room to work in, pad, pencil, a bottle of Coke and a bucket of ice. I had a stack of fifty dossiers to begin with; there would be more on the way. I had asked for the files on all personnel on the island, regardless of their rank or position in the company. By the time I had sorted those first fifty, separating the men with at least basic military training from those with none at all, and then divided those, winnowing out all but the few with combat experience, there was a tap at my door, and the clerk was there with another armful of folders, and just as well. In my first vetting of the files I had found only two men who had been conditioned under fire, and neither of them, according to their psychological profiles or by the type of combat they had experienced, was suitable for the job at hand.

An hour and a half later I had finished with the files and exhausted the possibilities. I had gone in hoping to find eight or nine men I could count on. I had found five. But five would do. Each was a well-trained, combat-hardened specialist possessed of a fighting skill eminently suited to the type of mission we would undertake. Each, if his psychological profile was valid, could be relied on to give me his allegiance in the job at hand. I committed their names and their faces to memory. I put their folders back among the dossiers in their proper alphabetical place. Then I called for the clerk and had him return everything to the personnel files.

I scooped a handful of ice out of the bucket, dropped it into my tumbler and poured the last of the Coke over it. I sipped and reflected for a moment. Assuming there were eighteen or twenty invaders occupying the island, my force of six men, including myself, would be outnumbered by somewhere around three to one. There was no reason why six men, trained and specialized as we were, and properly equipped, couldn't wrest control of the island from a gang of fanatics: no reason at all. But I was doing a lot of assuming and I was deliberately ignoring the imponderables, and those invisible little bastards will kill you every time.

# 8

I left my imponderables to their own devices and used the phone on the table to call Hajab. He was in a meeting but had left word that he was to be interrupted should I try to reach him. I was asked to stand by for just a moment. A moment later he was on.

"Forgive me. Have you found what you hoped for?"

"Pretty much, Minister. And now there are a few more things I must have."

"I am your servant."

"I think the less discussed over the phone, the better. I'll return to the ministry."

"Good. I'll have concluded my present business by the time you arrive."

He was smiling when I got there, standing beside a tray on a folding stand like a proud restaurant captain. The tray had on it a tempting arrangement of small sandwiches and condiments. He gestured for me to help myself, helped himself, and then sat down, with his plate, behind his desk. "I recall," he commented with pleasure, "that you said you would have the names of the men you would need by lunchtime. Therefore I assume it *is* lunchtime." He bit into his sandwich. I looked at my watch. He was right.

He continued: "You said on the phone that there were certain things you need in addition to the men."

"Equipment."

He put down his sandwich and picked up his note pad. "Of what sort?"

"Transportation."

"To the island?" I nodded. "By sea or air?"

"Air."

"Hmmm." He began to gnaw on the eraser. "Surely you don't plan to land an aircraft there?"

"No, sir."

He looked relieved. Perhaps he had been concerned about having one of his small air force's fine jets commandeered along with the rest of the wealth of the nation.

"Actually, what I need is a relatively low speed transport with some gliding capability."

"I could speak with our chief of staff for air, but I think he will tell me that we have no gliders."

"Not a glider. A piston-driven aircraft with enough range to get me there and get the crew back, and with some gliding capability. I saw a couple of old Dakotas at the airport when I was out there. Can your office, or some other ministry, commandeer one of them for my use tonight? No explanations to the owners."

He leaned back in his chair, looking greatly relieved. "You want one of the Dakotas, you say?" He waggled a finger in the direction of my lunch plate. "Finish your sandwich. Finish your sandwich and set your mind at ease. The Dakota is as good as yours. Both those planes belong to Petrolux. They are used as an air ferry service to Dhasai. They fly supplies to the island. They fly personnel in and out. Once a month they handle the exchange of personnel on rotation. I have flown to the island myself many times on those planes. Excellent planes."

"What about the crew?"

"A two-man crew. I know them personally. Most competent."

"Competent, I'm sure. But can they be trusted not to breach security? After all, you're the people who are so concerned about keeping a lid on the situation."

"I will speak to Mr. Boggs at Petrolux. Next?"

"You have no parachute troops. I hope to God you've got parachutes."

"We have an air force, Mr. Devlin, but those few pilots we have have not been trained as Kamikaze. You plan to parachute onto the island?"

"Not exactly. I'll want two chutes for myself: one back pack, one safety. I'll want one supply chute for an inflatable rubber boat—" I looked at him quizzically. He smiled back sardonically.

"We have a small navy as well as a small air force, Mr. Devlin. Had you wanted a battleship, we could not have accommodated you, but a rubber boat—" He spread his hands, then turned to his phone and made a quick call. He held his hand cupped over the transmitter. "What size would you like?"

"Somewhere around nine feet."

"Avon?"

"Excellent."

"Equipped with outboard engine?" he inquired superciliously, as if by his inquiry he were already one step ahead of me.

"No engine, please." He looked almost crestfallen. "That would be like traveling with a sounding alarm. One rubber boat with two folding oars, please."

He relayed what I had said into the phone and made a note on his pad. "Next?"

"Do your armed forces use Russian or American equipment?"

"American, of course, and ah—" He hesitated and fairly blushed. "Israeli. We purchase those through a neutral middleman, of course."

"Do you have the Uzi?"

"The submachine gun? Why the Uzi?"

"They're light and they're effective."

He was already pushing buttons on his phone. He spoke to a party at the other end and then turned to me. "We have the Uzi."

"I'll need four, and two thousand rounds of ammunition."

He spoke into the phone and made a note on his pad.

"Ask them if they have the Galil."

"Galil?"

"Also Israeli."

Hajab sighed regretfully.

"An assault rifle. A couple of pounds heavier than the Uzi, but adaptable for snipers' use. It should be equipped with an image-intensifying sight for night fighting. I'll need two Galils."

He was jotting as I spoke. Then he repeated it into the phone. "You will have your sniper's rifles."

"And grenades. A dozen should suffice. I doubt we'll use them except as a diversion. They go about their killing too nonselectively. Do the workers on the island wear any special type of clothing—any uniforms?"

He held up a hand. "Just a moment, please. I take it we're finished with the ordnance?" I nodded. He spoke into the phone, hung up, jotted a few final notes, and then turned again to me. "You were asking about clothing?"

"Yes. What is generally worn on the island?"

"No uniforms. Coveralls for some. Otherwise clothing of their own choosing. Mostly British suntans. Walking shorts. Chukka boots."

"I'll want an outfit of those for myself. I'll want one of your laundries to run them through a few times so they look like they've been used. Then I'll want them patted down with a bit of dust, machine oil, juice stains. Then have them packed in a watertight plastic bag.

"I'll also want a wet suit, black, to wear when I chute down from the Dakota. I'll be landing in the water, with any kind of luck. And I don't want white chutes. If white is all your air force has, I'll want them dyed. Black. I don't care if the dye washes off, once they hit the water. Which reminds me. I didn't notice last night, did you?—was there a moon?"

He was still writing on the pad. It took him a moment to finish. Then he looked up. "I'm afraid I missed that last."

"I said, do you recall if there was a moon last night?"

He looked puzzled. Then he understood. He punched up a number on his telephone. "We'll know in a minute. While we're waiting, you might review my notes. I am not famous for my stenographic skills."

I read over the notes. He had been very careful and very correct. I handed them back to him and started to speak. He held up his hand for silence and listened to his phone for a moment. Then he grunted and hung up.

"There will be a crescent moon tonight."

"No moon would be better."

"I am sorry." He spread his hands apologetically.

"I should have asked you to find out for me when it will set."

He smiled. "I did. Four-twelve A.M."

I was developing a positive fondness for Minister Hajab. "Sunrise?" I ventured.

"Five thirty-seven."

"That'll give me about an hour of solid darkness. It'll be tight. But it'll do."

"The flight by Dakota to the island is fifty-two minutes." He was anticipating me now. I let him know with a look that I appreciated his perspicacity. "As I told you, I have made that flight a number of times," he added, with self-effacing modesty.

"Then I'll want to take off from here at precisely three-twenty."

"The crew will be ready."

"And the equipment? I'll want the equipment at the field ready for loading by six P.M. I'll be there at that hour to check it out myself. I'll want a cot in a quiet room somewhere at the field. I don't care if the room is a broom closet, so long as it's quiet.

"I'll have a light supper at seven and turn in at eight. I'll want to be awakened at three A.M., preferably by one of the crew. Let's continue our efforts to keep as few people as possible aware of what we are doing. Tightest security all round. They must not know I'm coming."

"Understood." He didn't look up; he was still writing frenziedly. Finally he stopped. He puffed out his cheeks and let the air escape between his lips with a whistling sigh. He reached across the desk and handed the note pad to me for verification. "I personally will oversee the preparations," he said. I checked out his notes and handed them back to him. He extended his hand. I shook it. He held on. "One more thing. The control station is of vital importance. It must not be destroyed."

"Which takes priority, the civilians or the station?"

"Must there be such priorities?"

"I must take into account all the exigencies."

He sighed. "The control station." His hand went cold.

"Let's hope it doesn't come to that." I let go his chilly hand. "One more thing."

He reached reflexively for his note pad. I waved him off. "No. This is not for the record." He looked at me quizzically. "Assuming I succeed, what about the extremists?"

"What about them?"

"Shall I try to bring them in alive?"

"Of what use are they to us alive? The prisons are already full."

"That's not a very Christian attitude."

"We are not Christians."

"In that case, you may survive."

# 9

Hajab himself woke me, three minutes early, from a Nembutal-induced sleep. I forgave him his prematurity. He was understandably on edge. He was also carrying a tray laden, as I had requested, with eggs, rolls, butter, coffee, and a slab of lamb; I hadn't requested the lamb. It's a poor substitute for bacon.

I wolfed down the breakfast, splashed cold water on my face, left the tap open and stuck my head under the faucet. The water coursed through my hair and ran down my neck and back, but it wasn't exactly iceberg-cold, and lukewarm water doesn't really jolt one awake. I didn't dry off. I figured the night air outside would be chilly enough to do the job the lukewarm water hadn't done. Head still dripping, I pulled a T-shirt on over my wet back. A couple of hundred feet away across the dark tarmac I could hear the Dakota's engines wheeze, cough, and come growling alive, one by one.

I opened the door and looked out. The old bird sat there shuddering and eager and spitting blue flame out of her engine exhausts. I shook hands with Hajab and thanked him. He wished me luck. I turned and jogged across the tarmac. The air was cool and bracing and smelled sweetly aromatic, like a heavily laced rum-cola.

Inside the plane I made a quick survey of the equipment that I had checked in piece by piece earlier that night. Nothing had been moved. It was all there.

I took a short uphill walk forward to the cockpit; the Dakota, sturdy old thing, predates the tricycle landing gear. I strapped myself into a seat behind the pilot and co-pilot. Both British. Both young. Both formerly RAF, putting in their time until a place opened up with one of the big airlines.

"You're sure you can hit that little speck in the dark?" I yelled.

"We've done that run so often we could do it with our eyes closed. Why not in the dark?"

"I don't want to land on the island, remember?"

"I know. The chunk of coral a mile or so northeast. You want to come down in the sea just leeward of that. Consider it done."

"Let's go, then." He took the right brake off and pivoted on the left wheel. It was three-twenty when he swung the nose around and we began waddling toward the starting line.

We made our heavy-footed dash down the runway, wings flexing, feeling for the air, engines snarling— all two of them—and suddenly we were buoyant and airborne. No nose-in-the-air surging thrust, no human-projectile feeling as in a jet; just an almost imperceptible finding of one's element, like a kite breasting on an updraft.

And then we were winging out over the inky sea, a black void on our right; on our left a silvery carpet of light rolled out by the setting moon. The world was still. The engines droned slumberously. Cocooned in this venerable rattletrap, I experienced a cozy coming-home feeling. I had made my first jump from a ship just like her, a callow nineteen, spoiling for action in the closing hours of the last great war. God knows there has been blood spilled since then in the name of myriad hypocrisies and follies. But there hasn't been a battle worth a soldier's life.

Thirty minutes into the flight, I left the cabin and went aft to change into my wet suit and strap on my chutes. I lined up my gear in front of the escape hatch and snapped their release cords onto the overhead bar. I sat alone and waited. I was calm. I was ready. I felt a surge of excitement mixed with mild apprehension, a tingling high that most men leave behind with their youth, with first impressions, new sensations, the palpitating excitement of one's first encounter with a woman.

At jump-off time minus ten the moon slipped into the darkness at the western rim of the world. A splash of afterglow briefly outlined the profile of the horizon, and then the sea and sky around us went black.

At jump-off time minus five the co-pilot came back to lend a hand with the gear.

"We're right on course," he yelled, "and right on time. If you look down at about ten o'clock, you can see the gas flares burning. That's Dhasai." He plugged his intercom jack into a socket and checked in with the pilot.

I peered out through the small window, past the opaque density of the wing; we were traveling without running lights. The island looked like a festering wound on the body of the night, its smoldering, smoking, tortured surface an unmistakable landmark. No doubt about it, we were on course, and I wouldn't be dropped without a handhold into the middle of a featureless sea.

"Smoke?" he asked, offering a cigarette in the manner of a firing squad officer making concessions to the condemned.

"Wrong movie." I smiled. "I don't smoke. It can kill you in more ways than the medicos dreamed of. I have seen men in tight situations get their heads blown off after giving a sniper a perfect glowing bullseye. Besides, it dulls one's sense of smell."

He held up his hand for silence, listened to something on his earphones, and then shouted to me, "Hang on!"

The engines coughed a couple of times and abruptly died. The nose dropped slightly, and we were engulfed in awesome silence. There was only the sound of wind racing along the fuselage.

The co-pilot listened, looked at me, and then handed me his headset. I pressed one of the receivers to my ear. The pilot's voice came crackling through: "Two minutes to go. I've just cut both engines, in case you hadn't noticed, and put her into a glide. Old Dolly here may be slow, but she has it all over a jet when it comes to this kind of job. We'll be down at about twenty-five hundred feet when you bail out. The wind is behaving itself, too. About five knots from the northwest. I'll be taking that into account as I pass the reef."

I handed the headset back to the co-pilot and did a few deep knee bends. The co-pilot put the headset back on and began relaying information.

"One minute and on target." He kicked out the emergency hatch. There was a rush of cold air. The wind decibels rose. It was like standing at the edge of a gale.

"Thirty seconds. Good luck."

I wished the co-pilot the same. It is no mean feat to employ a Dakota in the manner of a sailplane some two hundred miles at sea.

"Fifteen seconds." He listened to his headphone. "Altitude correction. You'll go out at twenty-six hundred feet. We'll keep coasting until we're down to about a thousand feet; that'll take us some distance away from the island before we have to rev up and run for home.

"Two seconds; one second. Time."

I shoved my equipment out and followed it into the night, falling free at thirty-five feet a second, the darkness tumbling around me, molding my lips into a deathly rictus. Counting. Counting. Counting. Hoping that the old plane's altimeter was accurate and that I had indeed bailed out at twenty-six hundred. I planned to pull the cord at a thousand feet. But if the altimeter was off, if I had bailed out at a thousand instead of twenty-six hundred, I would never open my chute at all. Total disorientation in total darkness. I might be falling up instead of down.

I did a slow roll, looking about as best I could to see if I could locate my equipment chutes. Tied to the release line attached to the plane, they must already have opened, but they were nowhere to be seen in the impenetrable darkness. So much the better; lookouts on the island couldn't see them either. I fervently hoped that the capsules of iridescent dye attached to the equipment packs would break as they were supposed to when the chutes hit the water; otherwise I would be able to find them in the sea only by sheerest chance, or if they came down on top of me.

By my count I was in the neighborhood of a thousand feet. It was time to end my free fall. I prayed again that the altimeter had been accurate, and pulled the cord. A moment of nothing. A rustle of billowing silk. A hard kick in the pants, a punch in the gut, a chop between the shoulders. The mushrooming chute anchored itself to the sky, and the long, controlled descent began, down into a bottomless hole. I still couldn't see the water. And then, suddenly, more sensed than seen, the water was there. *Smack!* and I was plummeting through it like a lead sinker.

I pulled the pin on my inflatable vest and felt it swell and tighten around me. My hell-bent plunge began to slow, and stop, and stabilize, and then reverse its progress. Slowly I began to rise.

My head broke surface, and I sucked in air, lay back and enjoyed it for a while, and then began the business of hauling in my chute. It was heavy, tedious work, and it would have been a lot simpler to simply cut the shrouds and let it go. And probably it would sink, but maybe it wouldn't. I couldn't risk having it wash up on the island one bright morning like a colossal played-out Portuguese man-of-war. I would have to haul it in and sink it for certain, or bury it on the reef.

Where the hell was the reef, anyway? It couldn't be too far off. Just a couple of miles to the southwest, I could see the gas jets on the island spitting fire like a pack of dragons. I rotated slowly in the water, and there, maybe half a mile northwest of me, its low shoreline silhouetted against the light from the island inferno, was my coral reef.

I heard a splash somewhere off to the right, and then another, and saw, maybe a hundred yards away, the slow spreading iridescence of the dye marker. My equipment was down. Only then did it occur to me to listen to hear if the Dakota had pulled out of its glide. I heard nothing, except a pervasive hissing sound from the gas fires on Dhasai. If the Dakota had made it, it would be too far off by now to hear anyway.

I gathered in my shrouds, released myself from the harness, worked the nylon until the chute had filled with water, and let it sink. I unhooked the second chute and let it go, too. Then I breaststroked for the spot where my gear had come down.

I found the weapons pack buoyant in its watertight flotation wrap, pulled its chute in, cut loose the shrouds, and sank the chute. Then I sidestroked with my right arm, towing the pack with my left until I found the bundle with the inflatable boat. I gave its chute the coup de grâce, cut its wrappings, squeezed the release trigger on the gas capsule, and watched it unfold with a languorous sigh, straighten itself out, and swell up like a soufflé. I shouldered in the weapons pack, hoisted a leg over the wide, cylindrical gunwale, and rolled myself aboard. Then I lay back awhile and caught my breath.

By my watch it was four forty-seven. Fifty minutes to dawn. I dug out my range finder and took a fix on the island. Three thousand yards: somewhat over a mile and a half. The din from the island was incredible. I felt as if I were at the perimeter of a busy jet airport. On the island proper the noise must be deafening. Had I been aware of the relentless volume of the sound, I would have accepted Hajab's offer of a small outboard engine for the rubber boat. Nobody on Dhasai would have heard it. I doubt that they would have noticed the Dakota's engines had we not taken the hazardous course of cutting them. Why had nobody told me about it? I suppose because it was a fact of life on Dhasai. Living with cacophony on the island had become commonplace.

I cut off a patch of the iridescent oilskin from the equipment pack and flicked it over the side. I wanted to see which way the tide was running. The tiny square of fabric rose and fell on the gentle swell and within seconds was out of sight, moving in a southwesterly direction. And that presented me with a dilemma. The tide was in my favor, which meant that it might be possible for me to paddle to the island before dawn. I could risk it, but the hazards involved were considerable. If I didn't arrive just before first light I might arrive just after, and that would be the end of the mission.

The safest thing to do was to ignore the temptation presented me by the favorable tide and proceed according to plan: make for the reef, wait out the daylight hours there, and then proceed to the island after nightfall under cover of darkness. I would have to live with the fact that, while I waited out the day, one more hostage would die. On the other hand, if I landed after sunrise and was discovered, how many more men would pay for my impatience? I had arranged to drop into the sea near the coral reef for a reason. Waiting the extra day would cost an extra life, but rushing in precipitously could cost many more.

But even as I debated with myself, I was paddling for the island instead of the reef. Compassion for this morning's doomed hostage? Compassion was for amateurs. I could only weigh the losses and the gains. The hostage they planned to shoot this morning would be shot anyway, and the hostage tomorrow, too. It was on the third day, if everything went right, that things might turn around. How foolish it would be for me to put myself at risk of climbing ashore with the halo of the rising sun behind me, spotlighted like some saintly Robinson Crusoe. I turned the boat around and made for the reef before I had a chance to change my mind again.

# 10

I paddled around to the side of the reef that faced away from the island and dragged the boat ashore. I dug a protein bar out of the equipment pack and treated myself to another breakfast. And I was tired. The night was cool, so I left my wet suit on, pillowed my head on the gunwale, and stared up at the roiling galaxies. I was at liberty until sunrise. I would let first light wake me. Lapped by the sea, blanketed by stars, I drifted off.

I woke, slippery with sweat, pores suffocating in the tightly sealed wet suit. With sunrise the reef had become a griddle. I peeled off the wet suit, burrowed around in the equipment pack, and found my carefully seasoned British tans. I put on the walking shorts and a shirt and the chukka boots, dressing not for any reasons of modesty but to put something between my flesh and the abrasive pumice and the scorching sun.

I took a pair of binoculars from the pack and worked my way around the ragged little ridges until I found a chunk of rock that would serve me as a shield while affording me a view of the island. I was facing the northeast side of Dhasai, the high cliff side. It was like a blind wall shutting off my view of the interior and of the southeast portion of the island, where the barracks lay.

But the cliff appeared to be unguarded; no sign of a sentry or a roving patrol. Certainly they could not have been so foolhardy as to discount the possibility of an assault by sea. I panned my glasses across the top rim of the island and, after some searching, located the observation deck of the airport control tower, inland, sticking up behind the cliff like a small knob. They must have a lookout in there. And, elevated as he was above everything else on the island, he would have a three-hundred-sixty-degree view of the sea. I had been right to rule out an amphibious assault. One lookout up there could monitor the approaches to the island from horizon to horizon. Astonishingly, they had two. I could make them out as they moved around. Either they had more manpower than they knew what to do with, or they didn't know what to do with the manpower they had. Or whoever was in charge of the occupation felt that his people were inexperienced and preferred to have somebody, always, watching the watchers. Which reminded me: be careful. If I could see them moving around in the airport tower, they could very well see me if they happened to be looking the right way. My solitude was a delusion. I had to remember to keep my head down.

The sun was still behind me, so there was no danger of reflection off my lenses. I moved my glasses back to the cliffs facing me. They appeared to slope back from the sea at something like a forty-five-degree angle, were of a chalky appearance, porous as a honeycomb, and scalable. There was a narrow strip of sandy beach below the cliff. I decided that my surest unobserved landing would be in the lee of those cliffs, though my objective, the quadrangle, lay perhaps a half-mile south and west of them, out of my sight lines at the moment. I would have to wait until I landed and got the feel of the situation close at hand before deciding whether to scale the cliffs or work my way around.

I monitored the island for another hour, until I felt there might be some risk of sunlight glinting off my glasses. I saw nothing move except the two lookouts in the tower. Were it not for them, the island would have appeared deserted. I packed away my glasses and looked at my watch. It was six o'clock in the morning and the sun was well up. They would be shooting their second hostage. There is no feeling more sickening than to stand helpless in the face of onrushing disaster. I felt it now as I felt it years ago while racing to break a guerrilla assault on my home, knowing I could not arrive in time.

I kept the island under surveillance as best I could with the naked eye for the remainder of the morning and part of the afternoon, and still saw no sign of activity. Whatever was happening was happening in the interior, behind the blind wall of cliffs. There was no indication that they were augmenting their tower watch with a roving patrol of any kind, at least not along the shore.

Since the cliffs and beaches were not manned by lookouts by day, I doubted that they would be guarded after dark. If a guard was mounted after dark, chances were I would see him before he saw me, his arrival betrayed by the light he would be carrying to find his way to his station. He would have every good reason to carry a light, and no reason to suspect he was being observed at such close range.

I decided to move my schedule up by about six hours, a quarter of a day. I would shove off from the reef for Dhasai as soon as darkness fell, rather than wait for the hour of maximum darkness between moonset and sunrise. Triangulating my present position with what was visible of the airport tower, I estimated that I would have to travel no more than a hundred yards in the direction of the island before I was below the sight lines of the lookouts in the tower. If I shoved off from the sheltered side of the reef, lying across the equipment packs in my black wet suit, encircled by my black rubber boat, and remained absolutely motionless while the drift of the sea took me that hundred yards closer to Dhasai, I would be undetectable; and because I had arrived six hours sooner than I had originally planned, some hostage two days hence might not have to die.

Once I had landed on the island, the much larger problem remained: how to gain access to a compound which I knew was tightly guarded and make contact with the men whose support was imperative if I was to have any hope of successfully breaking the occupation.

I made a final check of my equipment and removed and buried the iridescent tapes on the equipment packs, leaving only the black waterproof plastic wrappings.

I set my wristwatch alarm for seven o'clock, built myself a bit of darkness and shade with the paddles and a tarp on the sheltered side of the reef, and went to sleep. I didn't know when, if ever, I would sleep again.

# 11

The wrist alarm comes alive with a nasty snarl. It has embarrassed me in elevators and restaurants once or twice when I have carelessly left it set and forgotten about it. But it does its job; it jolts you awake at the appointed hour, and no nonsense about it.

I woke to a setting sun and had something to eat while it finished its descent into the sea. When there was nothing left but a red glow on the horizon, I crawled out from under my tarp and, still keeping low, shucked off my British tans, packed them away in the equipment bag, and put on my wet suit.

When the sunset's afterglow had gone and the sky and sea had become darkly inseparable, I cast off in the rubber boat and lay face down across the equipment bags, but with my head toward the reef rather than the island, so that I could see where I had been and determine when I had drifted the hundred yards or so in toward Dhasai that would take me out of the line of vision of the tower lookouts.

The sea was flat and the wind negligible, and it took me longer than I'd thought it would to drift the necessary distance. When I thought I was within the circumference of safety, I let my right arm dangle over the side and gingerly paddled with my bare hand to turn the rubber boat around so that my eyes would be on Dhasai.

I cocked my head sideways and stole a look in the direction of the island. The cliffs, hulking and dark, were silhouetted by the startling display of light on the island. The place seemed afire. I knew it was only the flaming gas burn-off, but its fierceness still excited alarm. In the southern quarter there was a more steady, incandescent glow. And this I knew must be coming from the area of the compound. Midst all that blaze of light, I couldn't be sure if the airport tower was out of my sight or, conversely, if I was out of sight of the lookouts. But I was fairly certain that one thing was working in my favor which I had neglected to take into account: with the island so brightly lit, the tower lookouts must be almost totally without night vision. Peering out from the center of that gaudy arena, they would be hard put to discern any movement at sea smaller than a battle fleet. I doubted very strongly whether they could see a single black-suited man in a single black rubber boat even if he weren't below their angle of vision. Still, I was determined to be cautious; there was entirely too much at stake. I turned my back to the island, fitted my folding paddles into their rubber locks, and began to paddle, carefully, so as not to splash or stir up a phosphorescent wake.

When I had made progress of a few hundred yards more and was certainly out of sight of the tower, I turned the boat around again and rowed like a fisherman, facing in the direction I was heading so that I could keep my eye on the island just in case there should be any unexpected activity on the cliffs or along the shore.

Aside from the increasing volume of the roar from the island and the confusion of light, I might have been out rowing on a lake. The sea was limpid; the sky was untroubled. On long-ago nights like this, without the roar and the light, I had rowed on a cool, dark lake with my own sweet love before both my love and my land were taken from me. But it is folly to indulge oneself with dreaming of things forever lost.

A sulfurous stench drifting off the island reminded me that it was no lake I was crossing but a kind of river Styx. And on the near hulking shore lay the kingdom of hell.

An hour and ten minutes later I beached the boat in the lee of the cliffs and stepped ashore.

The beach was a bare ten yards wide, a ribbon of sandy pumice and stones. The hissing roar from the gas flares was incredible, deafening. Even with the wall of the cliff serving as a sound break, it was like sitting on the tarmac near a 747 running up its engines, the only difference being that a 747 will eventually take to the air, and the sound will begin to fade. When speaking, one would have to raise one's voice to something like a shout to be heard, at least outdoors. Certainly they had not heard the approach of my aircraft last night.

I used one of the oars from my boat as a digging tool and scraped out a shallow pit in the sand at the base of the cliff as far from the waterline as I could get.

Moving like a pack rat between the boat and the pit, I

hauled my equipment up the beach and buried it. I might move it inland after I had reconnoitered, but for the present the beach would have to do. A problem might arise some hours later when I tried to locate it, if a rising or receding tide changed the profile of the beach, or immersed it altogether. I had to mark the spot, but in such a way that the marker would be apparent to no one but myself. The simplest thing would be to take a fix on the stars; but the stars' position relative to the earth would change in a few hours' time, and I didn't have charts with me to help me to correct the discrepancy. Besides, the stars wouldn't be any help at all by daylight, and I didn't know whether I would next return to this spot by day or by night.

From where I stood at the base of the cliff, I could see a low, dark shape like the back of a whale some miles to the northeast, hardly separate from the sea, except that it seemed to be slightly more substantial than the water all around, and it did not undulate. It must surely be the reef that had sheltered me until just an hour and a half ago.

Some thirty yards offshore and slightly to my right jutted the silhouette of a small outcropping of coral or pumice. Its craggy cone-shaped top stuck up three or four feet above the surface of the water, like some shaggy amphibious beast poking its snout up for air. I fixed the position of my cache by those two markers, considering that the spot where I stood was at the apex of a triangle which included the distant reef and the nearby outcropping of coral, and that the angle was between fifty-five and sixty degrees. I had only to re-create that triangle, with myself at the apex, hours or even days from now and I would find my buried equipment. Unless the nearby outcropping of coral became submerged at high tide. A risk to be considered. But nothing is totally insurable against mishap.

I did a bit of beachcombing, found some large stones about the size of ostrich eggs and scoured smooth by the sea, and carried them to the boat. When the bottom of the boat, from gunwale to gunwale, was covered with stones, I dragged it from the beach into a floatable depth of water and clambered aboard. Using one oar (I had covered the other with sand where I had buried the supplies, to be used again as a digging tool), I paddled the boat out about a hundred yards into what I hoped would be fairly deep water. I lashed the folding oar to its lock so it wouldn't come loose. Then I unsheathed my knife, rolled over the side, and punctured each of the inflatable's seven air chambers. The little boat sighed forlornly and began to sink. I waited until the last bubbles had died, and then I swam back to the beach.

I peeled off the wet suit, disinterred one of the equipment packs, and took out my khaki shorts, shirt and shoes. I packed the wet suit back into the equipment bag and buried it. Then I dressed myself. I was ready to travel.

The cliff ran along the shore for nearly a mile, making a slow descent to sea level. I could scale it here and get a view of what lay ahead, or I could walk the length of the beach to where the cliff met the water. I decided to walk. There was less chance of mishap in the dark, and I would come out relatively close to the compound, which was my first and most imperative objective.

I could walk at the water's edge with the certainty that the wash of the gentle surf would erase all footprints within minutes of my passage. But I would be hazardously exposed. To any passerby at the top of the cliff, or even far down the beach, I would be a moving figure in bold relief. I decided to stay tucked in close to the base of the cliff all the way. I would leave footprints, but footprints were harder to spot and certainly more ambiguous if spotted than the upright figure of a walking man. Sometime before dawn I could erase them.

As I walked, I counted each step I took from the point where I had buried my supplies. Eight hundred and fifteen paces later I found myself looking out over the island from behind a shoulder-high escarpment that was all that was left of the cliff.

# 12

The compound, the objective toward which I had been moving for the past sixty hours, ever since my meeting with Heald in New York, now lay barely a quarter of a mile away. That last quarter-mile would be the hardest, the next sixty hours the most dangerous. I still had to penetrate that virtual fortress, undetected, and enlist the aid of the men I would need to free the island.

From my vantage point, looking toward the northeast corner, the quad took on a diamondlike configuration, with the two nearest buildings extending in a wide V away from me, and the two farther buildings converging in the distance, like a V inverted. There was an open space or alleyway about thirty feet wide between each of the near buildings and each of the far buildings. Though I couldn't see the other two corners, I knew from the aerial photos that the same pattern applied there. So that each of the four buildings was separated by a thirty-foot-wide alleyway, and all four buildings together formed a rectangle enclosing a courtyard which I estimated to be approximately one hundred fifty feet long.

The interior of the quad was awash with floodlights, as bright as an arena. An empty arena at this hour, from what I could see. I put my binoculars to my eyes and took a closeup look at whatever could be seen inside the quad through the thirty-foot alley between the buildings.

The surface of the yard looked like pulverized rock, light gray in color; pumice, I supposed. Under ordinary nighttime conditions, walking on it would be tantamount to sending up an alarm; the crackle and crunch would be horrendous. And I imagined that a good deal of the surface of the island, including the flat, open stretch of ground between where I stood and the barracks, was of the same crunchy material. Fortunately, for me at any rate, the ubiquitous din of the gas flares would render inaudible anything but a herd of charging elephants.

The buildings facing onto the yard were long, barrackslike rectangles, two stories high, constructed of whitewashed cinder block and air-conditioned by through-the-wall units, like a modern apartment dwelling. This much I could see through my glasses. I couldn't see the doors facing onto the yard at the end of each building, but I knew they were there; I had studied the blueprints. There were also twelve windows on each of the levels of the two-story structure, facing onto the yard, providing light by day and a look of domestic normalcy in this most abysmally abnormal of environments.

Curiously, there were no windows or doors on the sides of the buildings facing away from the yard, though the blueprints had indicated that they should be there, and there was the same pattern of air-conditioner units, twelve on each level, as there was on the inside.

The bloody pirates had filled in the windows on the outer walls with cinder block. I could see the outlines of the new work, unwhitewashed, gray as the island's surface. A formidable job. But considering the hundreds of captive laborers available, it might have taken less than an hour.

Bastards. They had had their hostages build their own prison, pen themselves in. Why, then, had they left the doors and windows facing onto the yard intact? Why, to keep watch on the chickens. Not only was the courtyard lighted, but from the field of vision afforded me by the alleyway, I could see that the interiors of the buildings were lighted as well. I suspected the drill was lights-on throughout the night. A shameful waste of electricity, but Petrolux was paying the bills, and what better way to keep the prisoners under surveillance than through well-lighted uncurtained windows?

With the rear walls of each of the buildings sealed, the prisoners had no way of leaving the area of their containment without first crossing the floodlit quad. To discourage any such foolhardy venture, there was a pair of sentries armed with submachine guns mounted on the roofs of two of the buildings, so that every corner of the yard could be raked with fire.

I had taken pictures of four sentries on the rooftops when I overflew the island at dawn some thirty-six hours earlier. Since there were still four men on the rooftops, either they were very tired, or there had to be at least four more resting somewhere, maybe in the buildings on the yard, maybe in the nearby cottages.

Through my glasses I could pick out a few of the small private cottages scattered on a shallow rise in the terrain behind the quadrangle. The lights were on in one of them. All the others looked abandoned and dead.

I could see the top of the airport tower, inland near the northern end of the island; and I could also see clearly now the two lookouts standing watch in a glass-enclosed room with a three-hundred-sixty-degree view. I wondered how effective their vigil could be, standing as they were in the midst of so much glare. I watched them for a while and noted that they monitored their three hundred sixty degrees in a casual and overconfident way, leaning against a rail, chatting while they peered out to the north, then the west, then the south, then the east—each point of the compass—for between five and ten minutes at a time.

Their method would not have been totally ineffective, considering that they were posted against the possibility of a relatively slow moving assault from the sea.

Figure a minimum of two more men to spell the airport tower guards who were not on watch: that brought my estimate of the total occupation force I would have to contend with to around thirteen. Maybe more. There remained to be considered the docks and the flow-control station. If they were guarded, I guessed at two men at each place, plus two to spell them. I hazarded the guess rather than risk personal observation, which would entail a trip across the island over open ground, or a long journey around the island via the beach behind the cliffs. I suspected that neither the docks nor the flow station was guarded, since there were no prisoners there to guard. Also, to guard them day and night would take four to eight more men. And that would bring the occupying force up to close to thirty. Even allowing for the type of international recruiting that these groups have begun to engage in, I didn't believe there were thirty well-trained fanatics in the world who could work together in a single assault for a single cause at a single moment in time. A twenty-four-hour day split into three eight-hour watches was a luxury only a regular army could afford; these people were probably posted twelve to sixteen hours on and four to six hours off. Figure then that they had a total force of maybe fifteen or sixteen men. Figure, and hope you are figuring right. Fifteen or sixteen men, holding five hundred for ransom, and beyond them a small nation and an incredibly powerful petrochemical conglomerate.

Five hundred men, drifting without protest toward

their doom. And all for want of someone able to kick a few asses into action. A rare commodity—leadership. Worlds die for want of it.

I decided to move my gear as close to the barracks as I could, now, while I had the chance under cover of darkness.

# 13

I worked my way back along the beach in the path I had trod before, sticking close to the base of the cliff, counting my steps. Eighteen hundred and fifty paces and twenty minutes later, a heavy trek through ankle-deep sand, I found myself at the apex of the triangle formed by the coral outcropping and the distant reef, and I began to dig.

I expended thirty minutes and a fair amount of energy disinterring, shouldering and hauling the first equipment bag with half the weapons and ammo back down the strip of beach to the observation post I had established for myself across from the barracks compound. I carried the folding oar from the rubber boat in my hand and used it to scoop out a hole in the lee of the shoulder-high escarpment. I mentally marked the spot, on a direct line to the alleyway between two barracks. Then I reburied the bag and sat down in the sand to rest, facing the sea, with my back pressed against the low pumice wall. I ate a protein bar to boost my energy level, put my legs into gear, and trod again the leaden eighteen hundred and fifty paces to my original landing point. As I paced off the steps, I noted with some pleasure that all the backtracking was doing a fair job of erasing the signs of my passage.

I dug up the second pack of equipment, filled in the hole, and kicked the sand around until all signs of anything having been buried there had vanished. I thought of disinterring the wet suit, too, and carrying it along, but I decided against it. However I left this island, I wouldn't be swimming. I shouldered the pack and began the return journey down the beach to my position opposite the barracks. Only this time I walked backwards, kicking away as I went all vestiges of my earlier footprints and leaving no trace at all of this most recent set. It took me an hour to make the journey this time. It was past ten o'clock when I finished burying the second pack in my little encampment across from the compound.

The lights were still burning in the dormitories, so that the guards on the rooftops could maintain surveillance of the prisoners through the night. But I noted, from what I could see of the windows in the barracks opposite the alleyway, that almost all movement inside had ceased. The prisoners had bedded down.

I sat down again with my back against the abutment and sipped a little water while I contemplated my next move.

As photographic reconnaissance had indicated, the quadrangle was well guarded. How good the guards were I had no way of knowing. But from the way they were deployed, making maximum use of minimum manpower, I had to assume that the group leader, the man in charge—this Woden, whoever he was—was very good indeed.

If I had entertained any thought of attempting to upset the occupation by myself, I had to abandon it now. As a lone outsider, there was little I could do except exchange my life for the lives of a number of extremists before sheer numbers cut me down. The situation would remain essentially the same. I might handle the guards on the roof without an organization, but at any given moment there were as many at rest, in reserve, as there were in the open. And there were the two men in the tower some distance away. My only hope of success was to reduce that force of dissidents to disposable size. To do that I had to adhere to my original plan: build a small fighting unit from among the prisoners themselves. Which meant I had to penetrate the compound and make contact with the men I needed.

Since all the rear entries to the dormitories had been walled up, I had no way of getting in except through the front. And that was as good as no way at all under present conditions; I would be spotted by the sentries on the rooftops the moment I entered the floodlit quadrangle. Curiously, I had a better chance of making my move by day than I did by night.

I could wait till dawn, when they emptied the barracks for daily muster. In the bustle and confusion of the early-morning turnout, I might be able to work my way undetected into the quad and lose myself among the prisoners.

Assuming I could successfully penetrate the quad in the morning, I faced one more immediate risk: if the candidate for execution was chosen at random, and I was in among the prisoners, the finger might very well be pointed at me.

I set my wristwatch alarm to sound one hour before daybreak. That would give me time to observe the habits of the sentries in the morning hours and, while it was still dark, to move across the open ground between the beach and the dormitories and to shelter myself in the lee of the building nearest to me. There I would wait until the prisoners began to fall out for roll call, and then, while the sentries' eyes were directed at them, I would slip in through the alleyway and meld with the crowd.

When I turned around again to take one more look at the building before bedding down, I noticed something that I had seen before, but the significance of which hadn't registered. The bottom row of windows—or, rather, the cinder-block outlines that had once been windows—were inordinately high off the ground. There was, in fact, on the courtyard side, a short flight of five or six steps leading up to the doors. Apparently the floor of the first level in all the barracks did not rest on the ground but was set up on stilts—or, rather, cinder blocks—some five feet above ground level. If I was able to work loose a couple of those cinder blocks at the base, I could move my packs of equipment in directly under the floor of the nearest building. What a lifesaver it might be, when the time came, to have my weapons available directly underfoot rather than on the beach nearly a quarter of a mile away.

I turned my eyes to the rooftop sentries again. For as long as I'd been observing them, they hadn't once turned around, hadn't once faced anywhere except in the direction of the quad. Why should they look elsewhere? All the prisoners were inside. Which meant that the guard atop the building nearest me, the building toward which I would be heading, could probably be counted on to be looking the other way when I moved the equipment in behind him. Reassuring, but— Since I could see the sentries on the buildings across the quad, their angle of vision must be such that they could see me. Their eyes, like those of their opposite numbers, were very probably directed most of the time toward the lighted courtyard and barracks windows. But occasionally they must surely glance up, out, or across, if only to ease the strain, and I had no way of knowing at what intervals they did this.

Projecting the sight lines in my mind, I estimated that I might be within their angle of vision for seventy-five to a hundred of the approximate six hundred yards I would have to traverse to get to the base of the nearest dormitory. It was my fervent hope that as they gazed across the brightly lighted courtyard, there would be little if anything they could see in the darkness beyond.

As an extra precaution, I decided not to make my move until that hour of maximum darkness between moonset and sunrise, when the light in the quad in contrast to the total blackness outside would render me practically invisible. I wished now that I had brought my black rubber wet suit down along the beach with the rest of the equipment.

I looked at my watch. Five and a half hours remained until moonset. I could sleep for four hours, retrieve the wet suit and be back in time to make my move an hour before dawn. Dammit, no! I was getting either tired or careless. In my business one never put off for the future what one might do now. The future was too much of an uncertain thing. I'd go for the wet suit now and do what sleeping I could later.

I got up on my haunches and turned around to make another quick survey of the quadrangle area. What I saw made the trip for the wet suit absolutely moot.

I was staring straight across the tops of a pair of dusty gray army boots.

I flinched reflexively. My gut turned to water. I had been taken totally by surprise. The infernal din that I had counted on to cover my approach had covered his. I didn't know how long he had been standing there. But there was no doubt about the Soviet-made AK-47 pointing menacingly in my direction.

# 14

"Don't move again or you will be dead." It was more an importunation than a command, almost apologetic. The voice was high pitched, singsong. English spoken by an Arab.

I remained quite still. There was a nervousness

about my captor that I found thoroughly unsettling. He was standing at the edge of the escarpment, his feet at the level of my shoulders, his weapon swinging in an erratic side-to-side motion across the general area of my midsection. He was skinny and young and frighteningly intense. His olive skin, in the dim light of the crescent moon, had a greenish cast. I couldn't see his eyes, but I could feel their intensity. I barely drew breath, afraid that the slightest movement might cause him to squeeze off a burst by accident. With his weapon moving in that back-and-forth pattern, it would cut me in half as neatly as if he had done it by design.

"How did you come to be here?" he demanded, his voice almost breaking with tension.

I strained to catch a glimpse of the safety catch on his weapon. In his anxiety he just might have forgotten to flick it off. From where I stood I couldn't tell, and there was no safe way of testing him. In any event, he was backed up by another youth a few yards off to the left. This one was also slim, small boned almost to the point of femininity; and this one also carried an AK-47. It was unlikely that both my captors would have been neglectful of their safety catches; and even if they had been, there would be time for one to correct his error should I be so foolish as to lunge at the other.

The second gunman moved a few steps closer in order to consult with the first. Not only was the delicacy of the physique feminine; the movements were, too, even under the baggy fatigues.

My captors were a young man and woman. I wondered if they were lovers, if they had been returning from a tryst when they stumbled across me. I could blame the hissing din of the gas flares for making it possible for them to come up behind me unheard; I could only blame myself for reprehensible carelessness in not keeping my head and my eyes constantly in motion.

The nearest youth motioned with the barrel of his weapon for me to climb up onto the escarpment. He and his partner moved a few feet back and apart again to make room for me as I scrambled up toward them. They were callow and jittery, like novice fishermen who didn't know quite how to handle a prize catch, but they weren't dumb.

I stole a look down at the place where I had buried my equipment. I had done a proper job there, anyway; the equipment packs were hidden without a trace.

"How did you come here?" the young man shouted again. He sounded slightly hysterical. But I dared not misread his temper. It could cost me my life.

Since there was only one way I could have come and I would be giving away no secrets by affirming the obvious, I gestured toward the sea.

They looked at each other, momentarily astonished, and then turned sullen, as if I had deliberately chosen to affront them with an absurd answer. The young man looked positively capable of murder as he shouted, "Do you think we are children? Do you think we are playing games?"

He motioned to his companion to keep her weapon leveled at me, while he unhooked a walkie-talkie from his belt. I glanced up at the rooftops. Though there were three individuals standing up in full view at the edge of the beach, the sentries on the barracks took no notice, continuing to direct their vigil toward the courtyard. It was of little comfort to me now to have proved myself correct in this one respect: the sentries on the rooftops were as good as blind to anything beyond the perimeter of the light in which they stood.

The young man opposite me pressed the transmit button on his radio and began to shout into it, in French, to Woden. I had enough knowledge of the language to understand what he was saying, especially since he was saying it at the top of his voice and with meticulous articulation, like someone placing a long distance telephone call for the first time in his life. My captor, who identified himself as Achmed, notified Woden that he had taken a prisoner.

Achmed snapped off his radio, replaced it in its holster on his belt, and raised his weapon again. I could see movement on the rooftops now. The sentries up there must have been monitoring the frequency. They moved to the edges of the roofs and peered out. I wondered if, even now, they could see us. Not that it would matter now.

"Move," Achmed ordered, and gestured with his gun muzzle in the direction of the compound.

As I was marched toward the quadrangle under the guns of Achmed and his companion, I noticed that there were now four men on each of the rooftops. Either Achmed's radio call had brought out the reserves, or, more likely, the sentries were changing shifts, which would explain how I had been bagged in the first place: Achmed and his friend were either just coming on duty or just going off, and had decided to take a stroll along the water's edge before turning in or taking up their positions.

Behind me, my captors had begun to squabble. Perhaps they were lovers. I didn't find the thought touching. They were growing distressingly agitated, and I was marching with my back to the business ends of their assault rifles.

Suddenly Achmed enlightened me as to the subject of their argument: "I should have shot you on sight," he shouted in English. "It would have been more easy."

I took little comfort in his predilection for the "easy" way. He ranted on: "No questions would be asked. There would be no blames."

The young woman spoke sharply to him in Arabic. He growled sullenly in reply. And then he shut up and gave up poking at me with his assault rifle. The young woman clearly had the cooler head of the pair. I don't know what she said to him, but I may well owe her my life.

We marched on in tense silence.

About ten yards from the alleyway between the barracks Achmed shouted again: "Halt!"

I did as he directed.

A moment later Achmed appeared in front of me, weapon leveled. He looked frighteningly on edge, as if he were the one who had been cornered, not I.

I glanced over my shoulder. The young woman was behind me, nervously pointing her weapon. Pathetically inexperienced, both of them. If I threw myself to the ground, there was a fairly good chance they would shoot each other.

Achmed's voice brought me back around smartly. "From which building did you escape?"

I could only gape at him in astonishment. That's what they had been arguing about. They assumed I was a hostage attempting an escape. Perhaps they had been assigned to guard one of the barracks and had been attending to each other rather than to their duties. If that was the case, the squabble may have been over the assignment of blame.

"You do speak English, don't you?"

I nodded.

"Then answer me. Now. From which building did you come?"

Tentatively I raised a hand and pointed to the nearest building.

Achmed grunted. He accepted it. Now I understood their look of bewilderment when they discovered me on the beach. Doubtless they were all alert to the possibility of an amphibious invasion force. But the thought of a lone man arriving on the island from the sea was so far from what they were expecting that it didn't even come into their consideration. The assumption was that I had fled the yard and found myself on the beach with no place left to go. In their eyes I was no threat; I was a rather pathetic fugitive.

"How did you escape?"

What could I say? "I simply walked out of the yard when no one was looking."

Achmed threw me a killing look. Perhaps he had

been the man on the roof who had been asleep on the job. As it turned out he wasn't. He unholstered the walkie-talkie again and pressed the transmit button and spoke again in French. "I have a prisoner with me who boasts that he was able to leave the yard because someone was inattentive," he announced reproachfully. "If you are awake now, there will be three of us passing through. Do not shoot."

As he tucked the radio away, there was an angry outburst from the woman. From the tone of her voice and the nasty look with which she froze him, she disapproved of the manner in which he had put down his comrades. They began to argue again, and so heatedly that had I made a sudden move they most certainly would have shot each other. But I didn't want that now. If I had correctly sized up the situation, and if I could keep my captors moving, they might provide me with that one thing which had seemed almost beyond my reach as I sat on the beach a little while ago: entry to the quadrangle.

Lighted like figures on a stage, we passed through the yard under the inquisitive eyes of the rooftop sentries and out through the opposite alleyway.

Woden was standing in the doorway of a lime-colored stucco cottage about fifty yards beyond the compound. He was squat and powerfully built, with an oversized torso perched on short, thick legs. His face was a bear's muzzle with a porcine nose, a short, dark beard and shaggy hair. Round steel spectacles framed tired, bloodshot eyes. A scholarly-looking bruin. He wore combat boots and camouflage trousers, a stained T-shirt, and a Walther pistol on his belt, and he was finger-feeding himself dry cereal, as if it were popcorn, from a palm-sized box of cornflakes. He looked as though he hadn't slept in days.

He sized me up wordlessly as we approached, waited until I was just beyond arm's length of him, and signaled with an upraised paw for us to stop. He motioned my two guards around in front to put himself out of danger of being accidentally shot by them should I make a precipitous move. He crushed the cereal box with the stubby fingers of his left hand and flipped it away.

"This is what happens when we grow lax," he said remonstratively. He was speaking to his gunmen in French. My guess was that French was the language of the mission because Woden probably couldn't speak Arabic.

He addressed himself to me in English heavily overlaid with a German accent. "You just walked out?"

I nodded.

"After evening roll call?"

I agreed, doing my best to look contrite. He was providing the answers as well as the questions, and I wasn't about to correct him.

He reflected for a moment, considering the possibilities. "I would say you hid below the stairs to the dormitory while the others were being marched back in."

I agreed again.

"You waited your chance and took it. You were fortunate. Had you been seen leaving the compound, you would have been fired on."

I nodded.

"This will not happen again. I will see to it that it

doesn't." He turned to the other two. "The spaces under the stairs will be sealed off in the morning. And there will be a body count as the prisoners return to the dormitories as well as when they come out into the yard."

He turned to me. "You think you are a daring fellow. You are a fool. Where would you have gone?"

I shrugged and tried to look ashamed.

"Resign yourself to a long stay here. Your employers in Behzat are not dealing with us in good faith. It is my feeling that they are not dealing with us at all. If things grow worse before they grow better, blame them, not me. I would as soon be gone from this Godforsaken place as you." He started to turn away and then changed his mind. He faced us again, staring through me as if I weren't there. "I *will* be gone. It has been my experience that a hijack that remains in stalemate for more than a week is doomed. We have been here for almost a week. We are growing tired; we are growing anxious; we are becoming prisoners as surely as our hostages. If we have gained nothing in a week's time, we will inevitably lose. I will not end this action in a prison in Behzat, nor will my soldiers. I will give your employers in Behzat three more days to see reason. Then I will move. My soldiers and I will leave this island. You and your friends will not. What happens here will serve as an example to the world. We will not be trifled with."

He turned to Achmed. "Take him back to his dormitory. And make sure you lock the door." As we trudged off into the night I heard him mutter in German: "A hell of a way to make a revolution."

# 15

*Abandon all hope, ye who enter here.*

The first thing that would have struck anyone entering the dormitory was the smell, like an uncleaned cat house in a rundown zoo. Too many bodies packed into an inadequate living space. Frightened bodies. Each one, even in restless sleep, exuding its own strong scent of anxiety. The curtainless windows were locked shut. The air-conditioners were running, but they had not been designed to handle such a volume of body heat for an extended period of time.

The ground floor of the building into which I had been escorted had probably once served as a mess hall, judging from the size of it, serving all the workers on the island. The floor space was occupied by row upon row of long wooden tables and benches. A stainless steel cafeteria-type serving counter ran almost the length of the building, parallel to the back wall. There was no food in evidence anywhere. Only bodies: bodies stretched out corpselike, curled up fetuslike, on the stainless steel counter, atop the wooden tables, underneath the tables, on the benches, in the aisles. Bodies shifting restlessly in the murky quicksand of the night, snoring, groaning, sighing.

Not all the lights were on; certainly not enough

light to read by, but light enough to see the bodies, light enough to monitor activity in the room from the rooftop opposite. Mess hall or not, I could see why Woden had turned it into a holding pen; the distance between this building and its twin across the yard afforded the sentries on the opposite rooftop an optimum view of the floor area inside.

A dozen or so of the inmates had wakened, or had been awake, when I entered. Pairs of eyes in heads upraised, like inquisitive toads, like drowners struggling for air in the roiling sea of flesh, studied me, appraised me; some stupidly groggy, some bemused, one with intelligent suspicion. He was one of the men I would need. I recognized him from his ID pictures in the personnel files in Behzat City: Jack Madison. Rigger. Eight years in the U.S. Marines. A Texan by birth. Had I overlooked his dossier, I would have singled him out now as one I would want on my side. It would figure that he would be. The others watching me were merely awake. Madison was alert. Apparently he was on watch, self-appointed. His vigilance allowed me to hope that there were at least a couple more of the men on my list in this building. Perhaps they had gotten together and organized a rotating lookout, just in case.

I moved off into a corner, found a small, unoccupied space, and sat down on the floor, arms encircling my shins, knees drawn up to my chin; there wasn't much more space than that. I waited.

One by one the wakeful heads sank back down into the morass of sleepers. I waited.

I had made note of the spot where Madison had

been, and could have approached him. I thought it better to allow him to approach me. It would serve as another test of my initial judgment of him. If he went back to sleep with the others, he would have to move down a few places on my roster.

I held my watch up to my eyes to check the time.

I noticed that the stairway across from me, which must lead to the second floor, had been sealed off. Boarded up and nailed shut.

The sound of the breathing became oppressive. It was like being locked up inside a bellows.

There were no more eyes on me now, sleepy or otherwise. All the heads that had bobbed up when I entered had slipped back and melded again into a featureless tangle of arms and legs.

The restless concert of snores and sighs continued, in somnolent counterpoint to the wind-tunnel roar of the gas fires outside.

The sour smell of stale sweat grew less pungent. Or, more accurately, my olfactory nerves grew inured to it.

I squinted again at my watch. Eighteen minutes had passed. If Madison had gone back to sleep with the rest of the lot, I would be grievously disappointed.

I looked up once more. He was standing, statue still, in the place where he had lain. He was a medium-sized man of stocky build, a solid cube of a man, formidable as a concrete block. Immobile, expressionless, eyes hooded, he watched me, waiting until whatever disturbance his rising had caused had subsided.

He began to move toward me slowly, gingerly stepping over, around, between the sleeping bodies, disturbing no one, making no waves: for all his bulk and kinetic power, an apparition.

I remained sitting, knees drawn up, back against the wall.

Madison stood over me for a moment, silent as a stone. Then he sank into a crouch and placed his mouth close to my ear. "I don't know you, friend."

The accent was American—southern or western—amiable, but with an undertone of menace. The implication was clear: I had better identify myself and explain the circumstances of my surprising arrival to his satisfaction, and God help me if he determined that I had been planted there by Woden.

"I'm Devlin. I've been hired to bring you out."

Madison looked at me skeptically. A question began to form on his lips. He scotched it. Instead he said: "I think we'd better talk. But let's not wake up these bodies around here. There's a john through that door, about fifteen feet to your right." I nodded and started to get up. Madison put a restraining hand on my shoulder. "The guards on the roof across the way can see through the windows, so take a seat in a stall. Take the one farthest from the door and shut yourself in. It's the only privacy left in the whole damn camp. I'll be along in ten minutes or so."

I didn't actually hear him enter the adjacent stall, but ten minutes later he was there. The sharp scrape of a match being struck, the nutty smell of cigarette smoke. A pair of feet. A voice.

"O.K., friend. Let's hear it."

I told him what my business was, who had hired

me, how I had come to the island, and how my captors had mistaken me for an escapee rather than a new arrival and deposited me right where I wanted to be.

His response was understandably skeptical. "You're saying you came in to get us out . . . and that you came in alone? Man, you'll need a small army to blow these sons of bitches out of here. Why the hell didn't the bureaucrats in Behzat send in a squad of troopers along with you?"

"There are political reasons . . ."

"You bet your sweet ass there are. Damn near half that country would just as soon see these guys in and those guys out. And where the hell is Uncle Sam? Half of us here are Americans."

"Uncle Sam doesn't know about it . . ."

"Bullshit he don't . . ."

". . . officially."

"That sounds more like it. Don't want to rub the right side the wrong way. And how do you know who's the right side till you see who comes out on top? You know why they sent you in here in this half-assed way? So if the shit hits the fan and we all wind up butchered, they can say an effort was made. That's the word they use to cover throwaway actions—'effort.' That's what you are, my friend: a throwaway."

"Call it what you like. But unless we make a move, we could be sitting here for the rest of our natural lives."

"And how long do you figure that to be?" he asked with some concern.

"Not long; Woden's getting restless. Which is why I need your help."

"What do you expect me to do?"

"You, and Stringer, Jennings, Fletcher and Scott."

"Where'd you get those names?"

"From the personnel files in Behzat City."

"I know something about a couple of those boys. They're the worst."

"I know something about them, too. For my purposes, they're the best."

"You wouldn't want to try to marry them into polite society."

"We're not in polite society now, are we?"

A floorboard groaned. Madison whispered, "Shut up a minute."

I peered through the crack between the door and the frame as a rangy, rumpled figure shuffled past. There was a sound of puddling water as he used the urinal. He finished and shuffled out again.

I waited out a silence of several minutes, relying on Madison's knowledge of the territory. Had I not been able to see his feet in the next stall I might have thought he'd left. Finally he spoke again.

"Son of a bitch didn't go out right away. He was standing over by the washbowl trying to hear something."

"You know him?"

"Douglas."

"What does he do?"

"You wouldn't want him. Polite society. Smokes a pipe and carries a roll of blueprints around."

"Engineer?"

"Formerly. Now he thinks he's the fucking village elder. How come you didn't come across his name in those personnel files?"

"I checked background and experience first. If that looked promising, I made a note of the name. I imagine his background didn't look promising."

"Damn right it didn't. Trouble with crazy bastards like Douglas is they take everything they know out of books. They never had to live with motherfuckers like these. You said you want my help?"

"Yours and a few others'."

"To do what?"

"Change the situation here."

"With what? Bare hands and good wishes? Those babies have got Russian automatics and grenades."

"I noticed. I also noticed that they're as jittery as kittens and not too heavy on experience. The two who picked me up . . ."

"They did manage to pick you up. What does that make you?"

I had no proper answer for that. "Take my word, all that lot have going for them is our inertia and Woden. The two who bagged me were more scared than I was."

"You expect us to take the motherfuckers barehanded?"

"I have weapons."

"In your pocket? Don't tell me they forgot to frisk you."

I accepted his sarcasm. It was a manifestation of his feistiness, his anger; I needed them both. "On the beach. Buried shallow. Uzis, grenades, Galil sniper's weapons."

He let out a long, low whistle. "Friend, I wish I could believe you."

"Believe me."

"It's a long way from here to the beach."

"I know. I just came from there."

"Under guard. How do you expect to get back?"

"I got all the way to the beach from the mainland. I'll get back to the beach."

"They must be paying you a ton for this job."

"I'm worth every cent of it."

"You get us back to the beach and I'll believe you."

"I'll help you. You help me. Where can I find Stringer, Jennings, Fletcher and Scott?"

"I know only two of them: Stringer and Scott. But you'll never get any help out of Scott."

"What's wrong with Scott?"

"Scottie's dead."

"Dead?" That was a stunner. I hadn't taken into account the possibility that some of the men I had chosen might also have been chosen by Woden, quite by chance, for his morning sacrifice. There was the scrape of a match as Madison lit another cigarette.

"They shot him the day they took over." I was still trying to digest it. A sixth of my force was gone and the fight hadn't even begun. "Douglas says that's what happens when men let their tempers get out of control."

"Whose temper?" I asked.

"Scottie's."

"Are we talking about the same thing?"

"I'm talking about Scott."

"You said they shot him the day they took over. They didn't start shooting hostages until the third day."

"You've lost me, friend."

"On the third day of the occupation Woden phoned an ultimatum into Behzat City. They would shoot one hostage a day until they got what they wanted. But that wasn't until the third day."

Madison exhaled a jet of smoke. "Jesus!" The smoke drifted up under the divider. "Is that what he said?" There was a note of grudging admiration in his voice. "Fucking bluff."

"Then what happened to Scott?"

"Tried to be a one-man army the day they took over. He jumped one of their boys in the yard; tried to take away his piece. Would have had it, too, except the backup cut Scott damn near in half with his AK-47. Dumb fucker must have been scared shitless; didn't take his finger off the trigger till the whole clip was gone. Killed his buddy, too. Damn lucky he didn't kill half the people in the yard."

"The two who picked me up almost pulled the same dumb trick. At least that makes one less of them to contend with."

"That's right. And there's one less of us. And since there's more of us than them, we could wind up ahead if we could get one of our guys to stir up a little ruckus every day just like Scottie did." He was beginning to sound bitter. "Is that your plan?" he asked. "Wear 'em down? What's the word the big brass used to use—attrition? If that's what you're counting on, forget it, even if you could raise enough volunteers. Because Woden learned something from Scott. They keep all their people up there on the rooftops now, out of reach. If they send someone down into the yard, they keep him well away from the prisoners."

"Do you know how many men they've got?"

"Not for sure. They never did a full-dress parade for us."

"Do they have anyone stationed on the docks or in the control station?"

"I don't know."

"They've got a couple of men up in the airport tower."

"You know that for sure?"

"I saw them."

"Then you know more than I do."

"Do you know how they schedule their lookouts?"

"I keep my eyes open. I see whatever it's possible to see. That much I can see. Eight hours on, four hours off. They change watches at midnight, eight in the morning, four in the afternoon. From what I could see here, I figured they had sixteen men. Maybe they've got twenty men. Then of course there's Woden. And then there's their own guy they killed with Scott. I figure about twenty men."

There was a sizzling hiss as he dropped his cigarette butt into the toilet bowl. "How do you like that? Twenty scrawny niggers holding five hundred white men prisoner."

"They aren't black."

"They aren't white."

"Neither are a third of the men they're holding prisoner."

"Who told you that?"

"I saw the personnel files in Behzat City. Scott wasn't white."

"You calling Scott a nigger?"

"I'm saying he was black."

"I don't give a shit what color he was, he worked with me. Any man that works with me is white. And whatever these bastards are, there's only twenty of them, and I think some of them are women. If we'd been ready when Scottie jumped that guard, we could have buried the whole gang of them."

"But you weren't ready for them. And they won't be ready for us. It's a matter of organization and ordinance. Pizarro took the whole Inca kingdom with a hundred eighty men. Woden took five hundred here with a force of maybe twenty. We can take those twenty with five. You said you knew Stringer. Where can I find him?"

"Stringer is in this hutch, if you're sure you want him. As for the others—what're their names again?"

"Jennings and Fletcher."

"Don't know. They might be here; they might be across the yard."

"Are here and across the yard the only places they keep the prisoners?"

"That's right. The guards spend their off-watch time in the building on the right; they sleep with the lights out in there. The other one hasn't been used at all since they took over."

"What's the matter with Stringer?"

"He was on my crew. As worthless a fuck-off as ever I've seen. Had to kick his ass every time I wanted him to turn to. High on hash half the time. Beating up on anyone who looked at him cross-eyed the other half of the time. I had to flatten him once." He added a little boastfully: "Maybe I'm the only man around here who could. Swore he'd kill me for that. He hasn't yet, but then our hitch isn't over yet, either. Anyway, I was going to see if I could get them to cancel his contract at the end of this rotation. You want a guy like that on your team?"

"He's a trained soldier, with combat experience in antiguerrilla operations. He's seen service in the jungle, the worst place to fight. He was decorated. He knows how to kill."

"He might turn on you."

"Or you . . . with a gun in his hand? Is that what you're worried about?"

"Wouldn't you be?"

"Maybe. I think his problem is that he's in the wrong line of work. He doesn't belong on a maintenance crew. Demolition, maybe. Swinging an iron ball. What I have in mind for him is more his métier."

"His what?"

"His line. Give him a gun and point him the right way and he'll do what's necessary. There are times when you need a man like that. We need him now. But, God help us, I don't know what we do with him after."

"All right. I'll find you Stringer. I don't know how you're going to find those other two."

He'd forgotten their names again. "Fletcher and Jennings."

"Right. How are you going to find them?"

"I'm going to ask. And you and Stringer will ask."

"I don't even know which of these stables they're in."

"We'll find out. Now you go back and talk to Stringer tonight. And tomorrow morning we'll begin looking for the other two."

"Fletcher and Jennings."

"Right."

"I think one of us better shag-ass out of here; the guards up on the roof could be timing the traffic." He may have had trouble with names, but he had a sharp awareness of the situation. "You came in first; you might as well go back first. As for me, I'm going to stay and take an honest to Pete leisurely gentleman's shit before the morning rush."

I found my way back to the small space I had earlier claimed for myself against the wall. It was smaller by half than it had been, thanks to a lanky figure sitting in the lotus position in the space I had once occupied. As I approached, he disentangled his long legs, crabbed sideways and gestured with his hand for me to join him. He was the same rangy fellow who had shuffled into the bathroom a little while earlier, and I doubted that it was by sheer coincidence that I now found him in my place.

I lowered myself to the floor, and he leaned close to my ear. "My name's Douglas. I'd like a word with you if I may, and then I'll move off and give you back your room."

I indicated with a nod for him to go ahead and have his say. He came on like an old schoolmarm.

"Frankly, I am at a loss as to where you thought you might be going." He paused and waited for a response. I looked at him impassively. He persisted. "Well, I must surmise from your dramatic entry under guard in the middle of the night that you had been foolish enough to attempt an escape. Where did you think you were going?"

I made no reply. I didn't even shrug.

He was not discouraged. "May I say that if you had been so foolish as to attempt an escape, you endangered not only yourself but all parties present. Now let's hope that the lesson's been learned and that all such acts of bravado are a thing of the past."

He paused again and offered me an opportunity to respond. I let the opportunity pass.

"Nor could I help noticing that shortly after your unceremonious return to the barracks, you chose to consort with Madison." There was no question about his contempt for Madison; the name rolled like something rotten off his tongue. "Now I don't know you, but I do know Madison. I don't know what your game is, yours and his, but I do know you're up to no good; and I must warn you, for the sakes of all parties present, not to provoke these people. They are not violent by nature. They are not intent on doing us harm. They are seeking redress for legitimate grievances, and it is simply our misfortune to be in the middle. While we cannot approve their methods, we can attempt to understand. We can exercise patience and restraint and allow these issues to be adjudicated and resolved by the proper authorities. I have personally spoken with Woden, and he assures me that if we give him no trouble, he will give us none. Of prime importance is that he not be backed into a corner from which he will have no alternative but to retaliate."

"As with Scott?"

He looked at me bitterly, as if Scott had willfully betrayed him. "Exactly. As with Scott! His violence begat violence. By precipitous and overt action, he made murderers of a group of confused and frightened men."

The man wanted squashing, like a body louse, but this wasn't the time. "You're wrong, Douglas. That gang out there know exactly what they want. You're the one who's confused. And, frankly, I'm frightened."

I got up and left the space to him.

# 16

My eyelids begin to glow red-orange and hot like the coils in a toaster. I tried to roll over, to get out of the light. A strong hand pressed down on my shoulder, pinning me on my back. I snapped awake, heart pounding, muscles tense, free arm cocked, heel of hand poised like an ax blade. "Madison!"

His square granite face was already drawing away; the hand that had pinned my shoulder was already coming up defensively, forearm set to block the blow I might reflexively deliver.

He saw that I recognized him, saw the tension go from my body, and he relaxed, even ventured a snaggle-toothed smile. "You sleep deep. But you sure as hell wake up mad."

The focus of my attention was beginning to widen. Bodies were rising yeastily from the sea of sleepers all around us, stretching, scratching, hawking up the phlegm of the night. A red-hot sunrise was exploding through the windows. A roar of toilets flushing in sequence, in concert, in constant and urgent use, emanated from the direction of the lavatory.

There was a man crouched down beside Madison, taller, leaner and younger than Madison, with a slightly off center face, sandy-colored curly hair and impassive steel-gray eyes. There were angry eruptions of acne on his forehead and his cheeks. His upper lip was smudged with a downy little mustache, and scraggly whiskers, like quills, sprouted from his chin. Neither the acne nor the whiskers had been apparent in his ID photo in Behzat City; perhaps the pimples had only recently erupted and the whiskers were an attempt to cover them; but with or without pimples or whiskers, he was recognizable as Stringer. According to the personnel files, he had an IQ in the neighborhood of 94.

He appeared to be every bit as unpleasant as Madison had indicated, with a nose that seemed forever to be dripping and a face whose surly cast seemed to invite a punch. He fairly smoldered with hostility, and I thought I'd best douse it before someone got burned.

"Madison tells me you're a troublemaker."

He threw Madison a venomous look. "Madison is full of shit."

"Then why did you come to meet me?"

"I've had the fucking island up to here. You say you can get us out: I'm with you."

"If you're with me, you're with Madison, too."

He shrugged.

As a concession it wasn't enough.

"Madison told me he had to flatten you once."

"I told him he'd die for it."

I glanced at Madison; he remained stolid. Then I turned back to Stringer. "Not while you're under my command. And you'll be under my command until every one of us is off this island. I'm going to put a Uzi submachine gun in your hand. You'll use it only when I tell you to and against whom I tell you. If you make a hostile move in Madison's direction, I'll cut you off at the knees. I have too few men to waste in self-destructive feuding. But if I have to lose one of you, it will be you. Understand?"

He knifed me with his eyes. "I understand."

I understood too, and so did Madison. Should we get off the island, it would be every man for himself. We'd worry about it then. Right now I needed the killer in Stringer. He wasn't twenty-five years old yet. And he wasn't good for any job but the one for which he was being recruited.

I turned to Madison. "What's the drill now?"

"They'll give us about ten more minutes to shake out the kinks. Then one of them will kick open the door there, like he was storming a bunker. The kick is just for effect. Truth is, the door is padlocked on the outside. If they didn't take the time to unlock it, they'd have to take an ax to that door to open it. Once the padlock's unlocked, the door swings as easy as you please."

"I noticed when they brought me in last night."

"He'll kick open the door and wave his assault rifle around very businesslike and yell 'Everybody out!' Then he'll back off the porch and down into the yard a respectful distance and keep yelling at us to shake it up. 'Step lively' are the words he uses, and he keeps waving that piece at us while we all fall out into the square. He'll repeat the same thing in the pen across the way. We'll all form up in rows of fifty for a head count"—he looked at me pointedly—"just to make sure no one's sneaked out in the night."

"How do they do the count?"

"What do you mean, how do they do the count?"

"Do they have you sound off? Do they walk down the rows and tick you off one by one?"

"Walk between the rows? Hell, no, not since Scottie. They're scared shitless someone's gonna jump them. The guard gets up on a bench and counts off the heads in each row, like cabbages. Doesn't take long when you're lined up like that."

"Then what?"

"Breakfast."

"Back in here?"

"Hell, no. You think they'd trust us with knives, forks, fire—anything like that? Outside! There's big cartons of Kellogg's from the storehouse. You know, those little single-serving boxes. The cartons are full of them. The same guy who rousted us out hands 'em out—really tosses 'em out, like feeding time at the zoo. One guard comes down from the roof to cover him while he does this. The other guards are all on the roof, looking pretty damn mean and ready, too."

"Water?"

"There's a well in the yard. We're allowed to drink from it."

"What happens then?"

"They allow us about thirty minutes out there; a little suntan time. Then it's back in the stable, and the padlock on the door till lunchtime. Unless, of course, they've got chores for us. The other day they turned us to sealing up the windows that faced away from the yard. Cinder block."

"I noticed."

"I suppose you noticed the stairway to the second floor inside the building."

"I noticed."

"Used to be able to go from the first floor to the second floor, from the second floor through a trapdoor to the roof. They made us board it all up. Might have been a little more comfortable if they'd let us use two floors in each building for living quarters."

"It also might have been harder for them to keep an eye on everyone; that's why they squeezed you into two buildings instead of keeping all four open. How do they get up and down from the rooftops?"

"I never did actually see how they do it. But there's a wooden access ladder on the back of each building. I guess they use that."

"What happens at lunch?"

"Same as breakfast. Kick open the door, roust us out, count us off, feed us."

"How do they prepare the lunch?"

"Prepare the lunch?"

Stringer began to laugh; a kind of sucking, hawking sound, like a rambunctious sea lion. He wiped his nose with the back of his hand. "Prepare the lunch," he echoed and began to laugh again.

"What do they feed you?"

Stringer spat on the floor and politely smeared it dry with his shoe.

"More Kellogg's," Madison said. "Sometimes it's a

different Kellogg's from the breakfast Kellogg's, but no matter which way you crumble it, it's cornflakes."

"Maybe it's loaded with vitamins."

"Maybe the box tastes better than the stuff they put inside."

"Same drill for dinner, then, I suppose?"

"Same. I tell you, we got to get out of here soon."

"When you turn out for roll call and meals, what happens in here?"

He looked at me, puzzled. "Nothing happens in here. There's nobody in here."

"I mean, do they send a man in to check out the barracks after everybody's out?"

"No. Only two men come down off the roofs, and they stay out in the yard. Nobody comes in here."

"You're sure? You'd see them if they did?"

"Sure. I reckon if the head count in the yard came up short, they'd do a sweep inside. Otherwise, no. Why?"

"Because if they do a head count in the yard and I turn out with the rest of you, they're going to come up with one head too many. I've got to stay inside."

Stringer diverted his attention from the paste of spit and dust he was working into the floor long enough to dart a grudging look of admiration my way. He didn't think too well himself, but he didn't mind allying himself with someone who did.

"Don't forget," Stringer warned, "those gooks on the roof across the way can see in through the windows."

I had already taken that into account, but I let Stringer think it was news to me. A little self-esteem might work wonders for him. "Thanks. I'll stay low.

Now you can do us all a favor during the thirty-minute walkabout you have out there, you and Madison. Pass the word that you're looking for Jennings and Fletcher. No reason why. Just pass the word that Madison is looking for Jennings and Fletcher."

Madison looked skeptical. "I don't know them. They don't know me. Why should they come?"

"What else do they have to do? If they get the word they'll come. Pick a spot. Maybe the water well. Pass the word that they're to come to the water well."

"Water well's no good. Half the prisoners in the yard wind up hanging around the water well."

"Any spot, then. You know the yard; I don't. If the prisoners like to gather round the well, there must be some place where they don't gather, some place that's relatively uncrowded."

Stringer cut a glance in Madison's direction and ventured a suggestion. "Where they buried Scott?"

Madison looked at him as if he were dirt.

"Did they bury Scott in the yard?" I asked incredulously.

Madison answered: "Not right away. They left him there, out in the open, for twenty-four hours, for a reminder, until even they couldn't stand the sight or the smell anymore. Then they picked a burial squad to dig a hole and drop him in. But in the yard, where it would always be a reminder. It's a reminder, all right. Nobody goes near the spot if they can help it."

"O.K., then pass the word. You'll be waiting for Jennings and Fletcher where they buried Scott."

Madison fixed Stringer with another look.

"Something wrong?" I asked.

"Nothing," Madison sourly conceded.

But I knew what was wrong. It had been Stringer's suggestion. The hard feelings between Madison and Stringer were no one-sided affair. Now that I had Stringer in hand, I couldn't allow Madison's animosity to cause a flare-up between them. I'd have to speak to Madison later, when we were alone. He'd have to give up needling the boy and accord him the respect due a comrade-in-arms or he might well wind up with a bullet in the back, and there'd be nothing I could do about it.

"O.K. I make contact; what then?"

"You tell them we're taking action for our own release, that we have weapons and a plan. Our timetable calls for us to turn the situation around tomorrow night."

"Tomorrow night?" Madison blanched, and Stringer began to look worried. Everybody likes his freedom. Nobody likes to stick his neck in a noose. It's much more natural to spend some time considering in the interests of delay. Delay long enough, and maybe someone else will intervene.

"No use waiting. Nobody else is going to do it for us."

"Will you want to speak to Jennings and Fletcher?"

"Do you know if they count you down coming back into the barracks?"

"I don't know. We file through the door two at a time. They could if they wanted to, without our knowing."

"Well, I have it from the source; they didn't used to, but they will from now on. So let's be cautious. You and Stringer go back to the opposite dormitory until the noontime muster. Send Jennings and Fletcher in here in your place. Tell them I'll be standing at the end of the service counter, in the corner farthest from the door. Tell them what I look like."

Madison studied me as if to prepare a description, and then looked flustered. "What the hell do you look like? You've got a face that you blink and it's gone from your memory. I don't know if I'd know you if I saw you next week. You got a face that don't look real."

"Tell them that," I said. "Or, better still, just tell them I'll know them."

# 17

Ten minutes after the dormitory emptied, the rats began to come out. Maybe they came out for the exercise, because God knows they would find precious little to eat. Maybe they came out in the hope that the good old days, when the place was a working mess hall, would return. At any rate they came out, deploying themselves like soldiers.

They sent out a scout first, probing, circling, scurrying back and forth, testing the room for smells and vibrations. I didn't see him arrive. He suddenly was just there, sizing me up with his mean little eyes, his nose aquiver.

I sat stone-still behind the serving counter and left the field to him. I wanted to know where he had come from. Satisfied that I was no threat, he did a quick reconnaissance of the service area and then poked his head out into the dormitory proper. Half a minute later he was back, sizing me up again, as if to say, "Sorry, old chap, but you're all there is that's good to eat around here." Then he scurried off again, about twenty feet or so, and stopped under the stainless steel overhang of the service counter. He sat back on his heels on the floor there, with his forepaws together in a prayerful attitude, and began working his mouth. I couldn't hear what he was saying for the pervasive din, but somebody could, because pretty soon he had a friend. And now I could see where they came from. Ambitious enterprise for a grown-up man: outwit a scout rat, trick him into betraying his hiding place. I watched as rat number two worked his way up through the floor like a furry gray plug.

They had chewed a hole in the floor behind the serving counter. In more normal times they had probably fed regularly and well off the leavings from the mess.

As I watched, two more gray-cloaked gents materialized. Now there were four of them, standing around their hole, grave as bankers, wondering if I was worth the risk.

They had shown me all I needed to know: a silver-dollar-sized hole in the floor. I had more important things to do now than to be eaten. I worked off my right shoe and then my left. Best disabuse them of any fancy ideas before they got themselves organized. Never let the opposition organize; always attack rather than defend yourself. I let fly the first shoe, right into their midst, and sent them scattering, about a yard off in every direction. They stopped and looked at me again, reproachfully, as if I had betrayed a trust or broken a contract in which I had agreed to be a complaisant victim. They squealed angrily, debating, I supposed, the wisdom of attempting to regroup. I let fly the other shoe at the nearest of the quartet and knocked him off his feet. With that they abandoned any thoughts they might have had about a counterattack. The three who hadn't been hit dove for their hole and disappeared. The fourth one limped a little and kept a sullen eye on me as he retired from the fray. He stopped and threw me a vengeful look before disappearing into the floor. He'd live to fight another day, and he wanted me to know it.

After he'd gone I crawled over and took a look at the hole. They had done me a service, my little gray visitors, and had been harshly repaid. I put my shoes back on and waited the arrival of Jennings and Fletcher. By my estimate some twenty minutes were left in the breakfast period.

Suddenly it sounded like Chinese New Year in the yard. Somebody had let go with a submachine gun. I flopped over onto my belly and began worming my way on elbows and knees around the perimeter of the hall, keeping out of the sight lines of the sentries on the roof. By the time I'd got myself into position near a corner window and raised my eyes above the level of the sill, it was all over but the shouting. I remained very still. The eye is drawn to movement. If I kept absolutely motionless, it was unlikely that the guards on the roof would see me. Especially in view of the activity in the yard.

The formation of prisoners was a ragged jumble. Some of them were throwing up convulsively. Others just stared in gaping disbelief at the corpse oozing blood into the crushed pumice in a clear space about twenty yards in front of them. The two guards who Madison said would be in the yard stood on a rough-hewn wooden bench near where the corpse lay, guns at the ready, muzzles sweeping mutely back and forth across the mass of prisoners. Their stance and the look in their eyes indicated that they were tense to the point of near hysteria. There was a third man, standing to the right of the bench, about fifteen feet from where the corpse lay, also armed with an AK-47, and from the look of him he'd used it: Woden was the executioner.

He fired another burst, this one into the air, and shouted until his face turned lavender. I couldn't hear what he was saying, but I gathered from his gestures and the gestures of the other two that he was ordering the prisoners to trim up their formation.

Moving sluggishly, like a mass of viscous proto-plasm, the prisoners reshaped their formation into a rectangle ten rows deep. Woden waited until the shuffling had ceased and delivered himself of what, from the working of his jaw and the belligerence of his stance, appeared to be a short, bellicose lecture.

The guards on the opposite roof were tense, their weapons pointed down into the yard. Woden dropped back about twenty paces. The two guards on the bench jumped down and retreated along with him. A terrible, apocalyptic thought sent a chill through me: they were clearing the way for a mass execution. They would cut them all down, like cattle in a slaughter-house, and I was helpless to stop them.

Suddenly Woden turned and strode away. As he marched off I caught a view of him the prisoners couldn't see, like a perspective from the wings as an actor leaves the stage, the emotional chemistry that has sustained him draining away. As he left the yard Woden's face was dead, cold, expressionless. He had vented his fury for effect. I had to assume that he had killed the prisoner for effect, too. I would have to wait until Jennings and Fletcher arrived to find out why.

The two guards remaining in the yard backed off to where a collection of huge brown cardboard cartons, like the effluence of a warehouse disaster, stood in a jumbled pile on the ground. The body of the dead man lay where it had fallen, halfway between the formation of prisoners and the two guards. One of the guards took up a position beside the pile of cartons, weapon leveled at the prisoners. The other guard slung his piece over his shoulder and, using a knife the size of a bayonet, began hacking the lids off the cartons. He shouted something at the prisoners, and, one by one, the first row of fifty filed past the body of their slain comrade and came abreast of the cartons. The guard in charge of the cartons began tossing out

120

small boxes of cereal, one to each prisoner who passed before him. As Madison had said, it was like feeding time at the zoo. Some of the men shuffled numbly by, their eyes on the dead man, not seeing the food box as it was pitched to them. A box was thrown to each man as he moved past, whether or not he chose to catch it. Most of the prisoners caught their parcel and shuffled off, shamefacedly, to the rear of the formation. The boxes that weren't caught, those that bounced off unresponsive arms or chests and dropped to the ground, were crushed under the feet of the oncoming prisoners. A few of the prisoners, by stopping and scooping up the crushed and abandoned boxes, had double rations that morning.

I tried to see where Woden had gone, but I lost sight of him as he left the yard. Then I saw him again, maybe five minutes later—although I could only guess at that distance that it was he—climbing a rise in the ground on his way to the airport tower: making his morning rounds, checking out his positions.

Feeding time over, some of the prisoners were turned-to, sealing up the space under the barracks steps. The others scattered about the yard in small, pathetic groups: broken men, ruminatively munching their ration, talking, watching the work in progress, shaking their heads, staring disconsolately into space. Nobody looked in the direction of the dead man anymore.

There were two areas in the yard that were unpeopled: a wide circle around the corpse, and the corner of the yard where Scott had been buried. I saw

Madison standing in that corner, alone at first. And then his solitude was broken by the wary approach of one, then two, then a third, not-so-hesitant man. The first two men who approached Madison I recognized from their pictures in the file in Behzat City: Jennings and Fletcher. The third man I knew from our encounter last night: Douglas.

Madison appeared to be arguing heatedly with the interloper. Finally Douglas stepped back a few yards. But he remained on the edge of the gathering near Scott's grave, watchful.

Fifteen minutes later the guards herded all of them back into formation again before marching them back into the barracks. The murdered man was still lying in the dust.

I did my lizard act, slithering around the perimeter of the room and down behind the serving counter again; the guard might come up to the door when the group returned. But even if he stayed out in the yard, I didn't want to be seen by the first prisoners entering. I didn't want questions raised.

I lay down behind the counter until, from the sound of the voices and the vibration of the floor, I guessed the room was adequately peopled. Then I stood up, unnoticed at first even by the two who were searching for me in that corner of the room.

Jennings approached first, his eyes darting warily from side to side and looking back over his shoulder. I would have to instruct him regarding that. They were good fighting men, these four I had chosen, but they were poor conspirators.

Jennings was lean, well built, red haired and freckled, and callowly exuberant. He even tried to shake my hand when we met. I ignored his outthrust hand and reached into my pocket for a pack of cigarettes. I pressed them into his palm. He looked briefly puzzled; then he caught on. Unlike Stringer, he was bright. We didn't want to appear to be new acquaintances to anyone who might be watching. He winked to let me know he understood, leaned back against the stainless steel counter and lit one of the cigarettes I had given him. He looked inquiringly at me. I shook my head no and took back the remaining cigarettes. I don't smoke, but I always carry a pack; they come in handy in the most surprising ways.

"What happened out there?" I asked.

"Man named Madison. Sent word around he wanted to see me and another man named Jennings. We saw him. He told us about you. I'm here. Jennings said he'd think about it."

"I mean the shooting."

He took a deep drag on the cigarette and exhaled the smoke. "Bloody bastards."

"Madison told me they weren't in the habit of shooting prisoners."

"They weren't."

"Then what happened? Did this man move on them?"

"Nothing of the sort. Someone tried to break out last night."

"No one tried to break out."

"Woden says someone did. At any rate, that's the excuse he gave for shooting the poor bastard."

"No one broke out. I broke in."

"So that fellow Madison claimed. If it's true, I'd like to know how."

I told him about the parachute drop and my trip from the reef to the island in the inflatable boat. "They found me on the beach and assumed I was trying to run. I chose to let them believe it. I was the one they should have shot."

"Not according to Woden."

"If I'd been in the yard . . ."

"It wouldn't have mattered. He wasn't the least bit interested in you. He didn't look up and down the rows for you. He didn't demand that the prisoner who had tried to escape last night step forward. He merely announced that someone had tried to escape and had been caught. And then he delivered himself of an oration on the topic of daring and its consequences. If you want to discourage daring, you don't punish the daring man; another daring man will repeat his deed. The daring man, according to the wisdom of Woden, is willing to risk the consequences of his actions . . . for himself. The way you frustrate the daring man is to punish someone else for his actions. This is a consequence he cannot bear. This is a consequence future heroes will have to consider before they engage in heroics. Then he reached out for the man nearest him in line, spun him into the clearing and fired a burst into him."

"Bastard. Has it given you second thoughts?"

"I'm here, aren't I?"

"Suppose we don't succeed and they shoot half a dozen men in our place: how will you feel then?"

"Sorry for them, but not guilty. Woden will have killed them, not I."

"Keep that thought."

He took another drag on his cigarette. "Do you sometimes have the feeling that the whole damned world is becoming a bloody free-for-all?"

I nodded.

Fletcher arrived: short, dark and wary, and simmering with hostility. "This pen stinks worse than ours. You must have all the heavy farters in the camp in here." There was no proffered handshake from Fletcher as he measured me with his steady marksman's eyes.

Like Jennings, he was a specialist, a trained sniper. Fletcher had been schooled in his craft by the American army, Jennings by the British. Both had won medals for marksmanship. Aside from that, they had little in common. Jennings had volunteered his services without hesitation. Fletcher, as I expected he would, had reservations.

"I'm just a little guy; there's no percentage in my fighting hand to hand. If you expect to take these guys bareknuckled, you can count me out."

Jennings looked as if he'd like to step on him. I held up a restraining hand. "That's why I want you and Jennings. I do my fighting at close quarters. So do Madison and Stringer. But we need two marksmen, men who can kill from a distance."

"Snipers don't work without rifles."

"I have Galils with image-intensifying sights."

Fletcher looked surprised. "You have these pieces here?" he asked, indicating the barracks.

"On the beach."

"A man could get his ass shot off before he got within pissing distance of the beach."

"I have a way. You'll have to trust me."

"Trust you? A guy who'd let another man take a bullet in his place?"

"He took the bullet for everybody here. At any rate I wasn't out there when it happened."

"I suppose if you had been you'd have stepped forward?"

"If Woden had been looking for me, I'd have had no choice. You can thank your lucky stars he wasn't."

"Yeah?"

"Because I'm the only one who knows the way out of here."

Fletcher fixed me with a look of grudging acceptance. "I wouldn't have stepped forward, either. Since they're liable to shoot me for what you do, like they did to that poor son of a bitch this morning, I might just as well go along with you. When does all this go down?"

"Tomorrow night. Go back to your dormitory after lunch today. Stay there till tomorrow. Tomorrow, after lunch, I'll want both of you to rejoin me here."

"Switch with the other two again, like today?"

"No, I'll want them here as well."

"No good. They count us down now as we go back into the barracks."

"I know. I'll have to get a couple of civilians to change places with you."

"How will we know them?"

"You may not. Just trust that I'll have two civilians in your place going into your dormitory after lunch tomorrow."

"You ask for a lot on trust."

"I may ask a lot more of you before we're through."

"What if you can't get the civilians to stand in for us?"

"I'll get word to you by Madison or Stringer that there'll be a delay."

"I hope you're as good as you make out."

"I hope you really earned those sharpshooter's medals, because if you put them down in your dossier just to impress your boss, we're going to be in trouble. Do either of you have any breakfast?"

Fletcher looked puzzled. Jennings looked chagrined. "I forgot. Madison sent it along. There were a lot of spares lying around this morning."

Jennings reached under his shirt for the little box of cereal. I laid a hand on his arm. "Just sit down out of sight behind the counter. I'll join you. I don't want anybody wondering why I missed my breakfast."

"You wouldn't have been the only one," Jennings replied, sliding down behind the counter. He patted his shirt. "I picked up a few myself. The poor blokes who let the stuff lie are going to be sorry when the supplies run out."

"We'll be out of here day after tomorrow."

"We'd damn well better be, or a number of people are going to starve."

"Surely Petrolux has a couple of weeks' supply of foodstuffs on the island."

"Surely they did. A cold locker packed solid with gourmet dinners prepared and flash-frozen by Martin's of London. We could have eaten like kings for the next month. So why do you think we're eating dry cereal three times a day?"

"Bloodiness on the part of Woden?"

"Woden's eating cereal, too, and it serves him right. The day those bastards took charge, they began pulling switches like demons. They decided to deprive us of our comforts, like the air-conditioning. But when they pulled the switch on the power line to the coolers, they also cut off the refrigeration plant. There was no power at all for twenty-four hours. Everything went sour. Except the breakfast cereal." He reached under his shirt and handed me another box of cornflakes. "Might as well save this for your lunch."

"The air-conditioning is on now."

"He had to give his own men some relief from the heat. He didn't want them dropping. He also wanted lights in the buildings and in the yard. So he turned it back on. You turn it on in one place, you turn it on all over. It's all on one line. But precious little good it does us. Too many men packed into too little space."

"How many more days of cereal are left?"

"I'm no quartermaster. But not much more, if you figure that the company stocked a three- to four-weeks' supply on the island, and we've been eating breakfast three times a day."

"Shit!" Fletcher plucked a box of cereal out from under his shirt. "All this talk about chow!" He tore the top off the box and began stuffing cornflakes into his mouth. "You say we're going to be out of here in a day or two, I'll trust you." With that he voraciously liquidated his reserves.

128

Jennings nudged me with his elbow. I looked up to find that a fourth guest had joined the party: a pair of well-scuffed shoes, pigeon toes, spindly legs; a rumpled tower of a man, gazing down at us with sensitive blue eyes magnified by steel-rimmed spectacles. His bony arms were crossed over his sparrow's chest. His stringy graying hair was sweatily plastered to his forehead. His mouth was turned down at the corners, evidencing his disapproval as I turned my attention back to my breakfast. After a moment he folded himself into a squatting position so that he was at eye level with us.

"Morning, Douglas," I greeted him.

He nodded to me and extended a hand in Fletcher's direction. "Douglas," he said by way of introducing himself.

"Douglas?" Fletcher asked. His mouth was full of cornflakes, and he chose to ignore the proffered hand. "Is that your first name or your last?"

Douglas looked nonplused. He was unaccustomed to having his efforts in the direction of rapport greeted with such indifference. He managed a smile anyway. "Last. First name's Richardson."

"Must be confusing as hell to have a first name and a last name that both sound like they've been tacked on all ass-backwards," Fletcher said and returned his attention to his cornflakes without bothering to shake the outstretched hand or introduce himself.

Jennings asked, "Didn't we see you out in the yard talking with Madison?"

"I'm afraid it was not one of my more productive conversations. Mr. Madison is not exactly a paragon of courtesy. May I join you?" he asked, politely if rhetorically, looking from Jennings to me.

Fletcher stopped munching on his cereal long enough to state: "If it's a freeload you want, we don't share."

Douglas, a past master at turning the other cheek, smiled tolerantly. "Nothing of the kind, although I imagine there are some among us in this hall who are bordering on the infirm and might have better use than you for that extra ration."

"Nobody stopped them from picking it up off of the ground outside, like we did."

"Perhaps certain events this morning precluded their thinking about their stomachs." He said this pointedly to me, but Fletcher answered.

"Then maybe that explains how they got to be sickly. A man don't think of his belly don't stay healthy long."

A wonderful group we had here: the one, Douglas, who'd had the grit for survival refined out of him, a man made of confectioner's sugar; and the other, Fletcher, so coarse you wanted to kick his ass. But I needed that crude meanness now. And so did Mr. Refined, whether or not he knew it.

Douglas's eyes traveled from Fletcher to Jennings and back again. Finally Douglas asked, "Which one of you would be Jennings?"

Jennings darted a concerned look in my direction. "I'm Jennings."

"What the hell is this?" Fletcher protested. "The fucking cocktail hour?"

Douglas was unperturbed. "Then you must be Fletcher?"

Fletcher stared back at him menacingly. Douglas smiled. "Well, no matter. What's in a name? I know your faces. One of you is Mr. Jennings. One of you is Mr. Fletcher." Jennings gaped at Douglas with a look bordering on alarm. Douglas addressed himself to Jennings's discomposure. "Nobody's taking names, Mr. Jennings. I learned who you were via the same telegraph that directed you to your meeting with Madison. And, may I add what I know of Mr. Madison would lead me to believe that you are all up to no good insofar as our present situation is concerned. We are adrift on treacherous seas. Don't rock the boat. May I remind you that our hosts are armed and we are not, and that they have done their best to refrain from violence . . . unless provoked."

Fletcher exploded, spraying cornflake crumbs from between his lips. "You crazy old fart! They've blown away two men."

"I repeat: they must not be provoked. If we remain passive, they will remain passive. They are a group with a legitimate grievance. Sadly, for us, they have chosen an illegitimate means of seeking redress. But let us remember, always, that their quarrel is not with us; it is with the regime in Behzat City. And let us remember, too, that we have been given fair warning by Woden. If you should take precipitous action, it is not you who will suffer. Others will pay for your rashness. Other lives will be on your heads, as was that poor chap's life this morning."

"On our heads? Not Woden's?"

"On your heads," he repeated. "It is our responsibility to behave rationally. Woden has chosen the only course left open to the desperate and the hopeless. It is up to us to help bring this grievous situation to as painless a solution as is possible. If we can keep our equilibrium until the matter is negotiated, as eventually it must be, we will suffer no further harm. Woden has assured me of this."

Fletcher crumpled his cereal box into a shapeless wad and asked, "You think this guy is sleeping with Woden?"

Douglas was unprovoked. "I beg you, if not for your own sakes, then for the sakes of the nearly five hundred other lives here, do nothing further to antagonize Woden."

He made individual eye contact with each of us in turn, looking for some sign of assent. I might have told him what I knew to be a fact: that the matter would *never* be negotiated, that the government in Behzat City would let us all die by the gun or by starvation before they would accede to the occupiers' demands. Had I been able to tell him what I knew, I might have turned an adversary into an ally, but I couldn't take the risk. I would have had to tell him that I had been in Behzat City only yesterday; I would have had to tell him about my mission, and I couldn't trust him to keep that secret. He might have felt it his duty, in the interest of protecting the others, to betray me. Besides, there was little to be gained from an alliance with Douglas, except perhaps his consent to stay out of the way. His skills and code of ethics belonged to another world, a world that was fast falling into decay, thanks to the careless stewardship of his kind. He was responsible for making extinct the very things he held so dear. He is an endangered species, he and his kind, as surely as is the snow leopard.

"May I have your word, the word of each of you, that you will undertake no act that might jeopardize the lives or safety of the rest of us?"

"Who the fuck does this motherfucker think he is?" Fletcher exploded. I placed a restraining hand on his shoulder. "Well, fuck him," he concluded and seemed to relax.

"You have our word," I assured Douglas.

"Thank you." Douglas looked satisfied and addressed his next remarks to me. "As I seem to have become responsible for the larger group of us here, I hope you will assume responsibility for Mr. Jennings, Mr. Fletcher, Mr. Madison and any others in our midst with the warrior complex."

I nodded.

He held out his hand as if to put the seal on our new understanding. I shook it.

"Thank you again, Mr.—?"

"Devlin."

"Thank you, Mr. Devlin." Grunting encouragement to his rusty joints, he raised his lanky figure to its full height and ambled away.

Fletcher whirled on me. "Some soldier you are. One sermon from that sanctimonious fart and you roll over and beg. Well, fuck you too, mister."

He started to get up. I laid hold of his ankle and yanked his leg out from under him. He pulled himself into a crouch and lunged at me. I felt compelled in the interests of self-preservation to stiff-arm him, so that he wound up plowing the floor with his nose. I held his head down with my left hand while I prepared to take Jennings's attack with my right. Jennings saw the look in my eye and restrained himself. He glared at me bitterly.

The scuffle had drawn attention. Inquisitive heads began to turn. The last thing I wanted was that kind of attention. "Now listen, both of you," I rasped. "I don't roll over for anyone. Nothing has changed. We move tomorrow night."

"You gave your word . . ." Jennings sputtered.

"Did I? An obsolescent man exacted from me an absurd promise . . ." I could feel Fletcher relaxing under the pressure of my hand. I let him go. "I had two choices: I could tell him what he wanted to hear and get him out of our hair, or I could quietly kill him on the spot. I chose the more humane course. But we may yet have to deal with Mr. Douglas."

Fletcher looked up at me with grudging admiration. "You're O.K., Devlin. You're my kind of man."

Hardly, I thought; I find it harder to stomach you than Douglas, which may be why I employ my dubious skills in the defense and preservation of his kind. You are the future. He is the past. In that walking reliquary reside the petrifying traces of so many things I once held dear: small decencies and gentilities, codes of ethics painfully evolved, all those things I once lived by and would live by again had I the good fortune to live in a more nearly perfect world. He is my conscience, whether I like it or not. I am his right arm, though he would cut me off if he could.

# 18

The hall emptied for lunch and I was alone again. Jennings had left me an extra box of food; I wolfed it down and then set to work to prepare for the irrevocable step that the five of us would take the next night.

I wouldn't see Jennings or Fletcher until then. I hoped that Fletcher would hold his tongue and his temper and not precipitate another shooting incident in which he might very well become the third victim of our benevolent captors. In the meantime I had work to do: I had to prepare our exit route, a job that could be undertaken only during feeding times, when the hall was emptied of prisoners. I would also have to arrange for Madison to persuade two trustworthy civilians to take the places of Jennings and Fletcher in the other dormitory after tomorrow night's dinner call.

On my belly I wormed my way around the room, keeping my flank glued to the wall, lying still as a stone when the sentries on the opposite roof were looking in my direction, moving on when their eyes were turned away.

It took me a full five minutes to negotiate the negligible distance between the back of the serving counter and the washroom. There, nose down in the soil and stench, I worked my way along the linoleum floor until I found shelter beneath the sinks. I rolled over onto my back, looked up, and found what I was looking for.

A steel rod approximately sixteen inches in length operates the drain in the sink. To liberate it I had only to remove a pair of nuts and bolts.

I wrapped my handkerchief around my hand to protect the tips of my fingers and set to work.

A little patience, a little pain; a split nail on the right index finger, a bloody thumb, and the job was finished. I reached up over the lip of the sink, took hold of the drain head and carefully drew it out, and the rod along with it. I tucked it under my belt and worked my way back around the room and behind the service counter. The meal period was twenty minutes gone; I had approximately ten minutes of working time remaining before the prisoners returned.

I crawled under the overhang at the back of the serving counter and found the jagged little dollar-sized hole that the rats had opened in the floorboard; without it I would have been hard put to find a place of purchase for my lever.

I slipped the steel drain rod into the rathole to a depth of about six inches, that left me ten inches of "handle" sticking up at an angle of about sixty degrees. "Give me a lever," Archimedes once said, "and a place to stand, and I can move the world." Well, I dared not stand; I had to work out of a crouch, but then I wasn't trying to move the world: just a piece of pine flooring about four inches wide and three feet long for starters.

I laid both hands along the top of the rod, took a deep breath, straightened my back, and bore down

136

with steady pressure and all the force I could muster. There was a mournful groan, as if the wood were in pain, as the nails in the floorboard reluctantly released their grip on the joists. I sat back on my haunches and surveyed what I had done. The board had been raised about two inches at the levered end, and the nails that had held it down were exposed now and merely resting, like a pair of silvered fangs, on the underbeam.

I moved my lever down the length of the board and laid my weight on it again. There was another groan—more resigned than the first, it seemed—as the far end of the board began to lift.

I wedged the lever into the last angle of resistance at the farthest end of the plank and bore down again; with something like a sigh, the board came free. I laid it aside, dropped flat on my belly, and peered down through the four-inch-wide gap I had opened in the floor. There was a strong smell of rat shit, but very little to see; the cinder-block wall all around effectively blacked out the cellar. Aside from a few vagrant streaks of light filtering through eroded places in the mortar, the space under the dormitory lay in musty darkness. I could see a small, rectangular area directly below me which was illuminated by the beam of light coming through the opening I had made in the floor; it revealed only that the surface beneath the building was unfinished: a pitted, irregular gritty footing.

I picked up the board that I had removed and turned it over on its back, carpenter's nails up. I laid it across the opening; and, using the head of the drain rod as a mallet, I knocked the nails out of the board, careful to catch and pocket them before they could drop into the sand below. One never knew to what good use a two-inch steel nail might be put, even a slightly bent one.

I looked at my watch. Five minutes remained before the prisoners would return. I pried up a second board in much the same manner as the first, but with slightly more difficulty; with the increasing width of the space between the floorboards, my fulcrum was losing its effectiveness. I set the board aside and measured what I had done. I now had an opening in the floor approximately eight inches wide and three feet long. I would have to pry loose at least two more boards to make a space wide enough for a man to drop through. And to do that I would need a longer lever than I had in my drain rod.

I hammered the nails out of the second board and pocketed them. Then I fitted both boards back into their original places in the floor. Since the two freed boards were situated under the overhang of the counter, the likelihood of their being jarred loose by foot traffic was remote. Still, I would have to see to it that either Madison, Stringer or myself was sitting across those boards at all times.

I was still looking for a safe place to store the drain rod when the door to the building banged open. There was a buzz of voices and a shuffling of feet as the prisoners began filing back in.

With one of the nails from the floorboard, I punched a hole in the left side pocket of my trousers. I slipped the rod into the pocket, down through the hole, until its progress was arrested by its broad, flat top. There it hung like a sheathed sword against my thigh.

# 19

That evening, while the prisoners were out in the yard, I returned to work on the opening in the floor. I lifted out the two boards I had pried up earlier in the day, set them aside, and fitted the end of the drain rod under the next secure board in line. But the drain rod was only sixteen inches long and the space I had already opened was eight inches wide; my fulcrum was at the center point of my lever.

I bore down on the rod and proved to myself what I had already suspected: I hadn't enough leverage to lift the third board. And I would have to lift at least two more boards if we were to get down through that hole. My progress mocked me: the space I had already opened made a wider opening impossible. There was nothing to do but undo what I had so painstakingly done: put everything back as it had been and start all over again when I had a proper tool. Perhaps not until morning.

In forty-eight hours Woden would make good his threat to waste the island and everyone on it, and I might lose half a day for want of a lever. I set the first board carefully in its place and was preparing to secure it with the nails when I noticed something I should have seen much sooner. With the first board back in place, there was only a four-inch gap to be spanned to reach board number three. Easy work for my lever. After prying up board number three, all I'd need do was to replace board number two and, from that platform, attack board number four. Working this way, I could remove the whole floor if I chose to.

Ten minutes later I had two more boards lifted and stripped of their nails. The opening in the floor was just wide enough for a man to drop through. A tempting proposition.

In the time remaining before the prisoners returned, I could lower myself through the opening in the floor and make a quick reconnaissance of the airway beneath the building. But without assistance I might not be able to come up. I might find myself trapped down there, and for what? To satisfy my curiosity? To put a damper on my restlessness? There would be time later for that. Judging from the situation of the first floor, there was approximately five feet of headroom in the hot, musty cellar. Once I was down there, the floor above my head would be shoulder high. The opening in the floor was wide enough to drop through, but it would not afford a lone man enough maneuvering space to haul himself up unaided. I might be unable to come up until the prisoners in the yard returned. And that was the last thing I wanted. There were hours of work to be done in the space below the floor before we could make our escape, but this was not the time to begin. We would begin at night, when the others were asleep, when there would be three of us to ensure security and mobility.

I fitted the loose floorboards back into place.

Surveying my work, I leaned back against the inside wall of the service counter and was seized by an involuntary shudder. The wall was cool, my shirt was clammy, and my back was bathed in sweat.

# 20

How did we know it was night? Because it was brighter than day outside in the floodlit yard; because it had been five hours since the prisoners had had their evening meal; because the barracks was no longer abuzz with voices. The continuous flushing of the toilets had abated. Two hundred forty-odd bodies had settled down to sleep.

Someone groaned, someone snored, someone turned over; a floorboard creaked. In a corner of the room someone muffled a sob into a balled-up shirt; somewhere else in the darkness someone muttered a prayer. And dominating all sounds, the roar of the gas flares; muted by sealed windows and the air-conditioner's hum, but ever with us.

Behind the service counter Madison assured me that present conditions were as good as we could expect for our trip below. There were a couple of bodies sprawled behind the counter some yards from us. We had been monitoring their breathing and their movements for a quarter of an hour; they were dead to the world.

Stringer had the lookout. Madison and I would go

below to do what had to be done if we were to make our move on the following night.

On my signal Stringer and Madison moved into sitting positions, shoulder to shoulder, side by side, forming as best they could a blind behind which I could work, safe from prying eyes should anyone on our side of the room waken.

Lying on my belly, I carefully lifted out the floorboards that I had prepared for easy removal earlier in the day. It would be Stringer's job to replace them once we were down.

I sat up with my back to Stringer and Madison and my legs dangling through the gap in the floor. I braced my hands on the lip of the hole and prepared to shove off—and checked my movement just in time. I felt the steel spine of the drain rod pressing against my thigh under my trousers. I slipped it out of the makeshift sheath in my pocket and set it down beside the opening in the floor; I didn't want to wind up with a couple of inches of it in my gut after a five-foot drop into the sand below. I set the carpenter's nails down beside the rod, nudged Madison, and asked him to hand it all down to me before he jumped. I took a quick look around to make sure all the sleepers in sight were still sleeping, and then I shoved off.

I landed on the wrong side of a hard little mound of crushed pumice and pitched over onto my back. I let myself roll to absorb the impact. No harm done. I shook the cobwebs out of my head and the grit out of my hair. I looked up and saw Madison's feet dangling through the hole, and it occurred to me belatedly that I should have let him go first. It was a simple matter of priorities. Had there been a pile of cast-off cinder blocks down there instead of sand, I might have broken an ankle—or worse—and I was the only one who could locate the cache of weapons buried on the beach.

I signaled Madison to wait while I kicked the mound of earth that had tripped me up. I broke it up with my shoe and flattened it out. Then I reached up and took the steel rod and the nails from him and got out of the way. Madison came thudding down, and Stringer's face appeared in the opening in the floor, looking in to see if everything was all right. I signaled him that we were O.K., and he began to fill in the hole in the floor above us, board by board.

I dropped into a crouch beside Madison as the last boards were fitted into place. We would do the rest of the night's work on our knees, or risk fracturing our skulls on the low overhead should we venture to stand upright in the darkness. And darkness there was, in abundance. Vagrant streaks of light slitting through the floorboards above and through fissures in the mortar on the yard side of the building were stamped in crazy patterns on the ground, like tracer-bullet tracks slicing randomly through the blackness: not enough light to illuminate anything but enough to destroy night vision. The back wall, the wall facing the sea, the wall on which we would be working, was invisible. We crawled through the tracer tracks toward the darkness. It was like reeling through a blackout with strobe lights flashing in our eyes. The effect was dizzying. Finally, we simply closed our eyes.

Groping the air like blind men, we found the wall and set to work, tactilely, locating the mortared outlines of the cinder blocks. Then, working with the carpenter's nails that I had taken from the floorboards earlier in the day, we began to scrape away the cement.

Walls and doors are merely symbols, trappings of polite society. They demark property. They are a sign that says "All within is mine." In a civilized world they have meaning because civilized men respect the things they stand for: privacy and property. But they are not inviolate. Locks can be blown, gates unhinged, bricks removed one by one. I know. I have seen what happens in a savage world. A wall means nothing to me.

Like moles, Madison and I scratched away in the darkness with carpenter's nails on the dry cement. Our goal, before the night was through, was to remove the mortar from around three cinder blocks—two below, one above—so that on the next night, when the time came to go, we could simply shove them out of their places in the wall and open up a hole large enough for a man to crawl through. Our enterprise was something like attempting to empty a bathtubful of water with an eyedropper.

Tools slipped. Knuckles skidded on rough stone. In an hour's time our fingers were raw meat, oozing blood. It had been our plan to work at the cinder block for a maximum of five hours, until just before dawn, before the other prisoners wakened. We soon knew that five hours would not be enough.

You must realize that employing a two-inch carpenter's nail to ream out the seams in a heavy cinder block poses some special problems. After we had scraped out mortar to the depth of an inch, leaving an inch of nail as a handle, we began to lose our purchase on the tool. Muscle cramps curled and crippled our fingers; our wrists and forearms seized up arthritically in pain. We were forced at increasingly frequent intervals to stop, to flex our fingers and work life back into our petrifying limbs.

We decided that in order to continue we would have to reduce the thickness of the cinder block as we made progress on the seam; we would have to scoop it out like a stone melon.

We decided that if we failed to finish the job by dawn, I would stay below alone and work throughout the day. No one would miss me, since no one was aware of my presence.

At two o'clock in the morning we discovered what every bricklayer knows: cinder blocks are hollow. We broke through the inner face into the hollow core. Suddenly we were halfway home.

Whereas earlier we had despaired of ever breaking through, we now became concerned with penetrating the outer wall prematurely. We weren't ready to go tonight. If the wall was holed and Woden or one of his sentries passed close to the seaward side of the building during the day, our escape would be blown.

At three o'clock in the morning a premature break-through became the least of our concerns.

A sudden cascade of light spilling in from above and behind us spun us around. Someone was removing, one by one, the boards that covered our opening in the floor.

145

Squinting painfully into the dazzling brightness, I gripped the steel drain rod clublike in my fist. It was the only weapon we had.

Perhaps the intruder was a lone inquisitive guard who had been spending an off-duty hour lounging just outside the wall where we were working. Perhaps he had heard the persistent scraping and decided to investigate. If that was the case, how had he found our hole, and what had become of Stringer?

The third of the floorboards was being lifted away. Where was Stringer?

Stealthily I began to move up close to the brilliant golden rectangle of light projected through the hole in the floor above. I had decided that if the guard poked his head down and flicked on a flashlight, I would club him with the drain rod, stun him, drag him down, and finish him off in the darkness. We would have to deal with the consequences later. If he saw us and reported us, everything would be lost anyway.

If he was not alone, if there was a squad of them up there with him, then we would have bought it. But at least we would have taken the fighting chance. And since they would have vented their fury directly upon us, the likelihood of reprisals against the innocent would have been minimized. The fourth floorboard was lifted out.

The rectangle of light was momentarily eclipsed as a torso spread itself across the opening in the floor. I raised the steel rod and waited.

No man's head appeared, nor did a flashlight.

The body dropped like a sandbag and smacked with a fruity thump into the sand at my feet. I started to swing the steel rod and checked myself. Madison had leaped as the man dropped and landed across his chest; I might have brained Madison.

The intruder lay flat on his back in the bright rectangle, agape, staring straight up, unblinking, into the light. It was Douglas.

A moment later Stringer's head and shoulders moved into the frame. I stepped into the lighted area so that Stringer could see me.

"What the hell happened?" I rasped.

"I cold-cocked him."

"I can see that."

"He was going to blow the whistle."

"How do you know?"

"He told me."

"His kind always do."

"Blow the whistle?"

"Run off at the mouth to their own disadvantage."

"He said he'd been watching you, and he knew you were up to something; 'up to no good' is what he said. He wanted me to tell him where you'd gone, or he was going to call a guard. You understand? He was going to call a guard. I told him O.K.; I'd let him talk it over with you. I didn't know what else to do. You understand? I started to take the boards away. When he leaned over to look down, I chopped him and let him drop."

"Dumb kid. I knew he'd screw up." It was Madison, standing at my side, fairly gloating. I ordered him to shut up before he made things worse.

Douglas groaned like a man badly hung over and turned his face away from the light.

"Did I kill him?"

"I doubt it."

Douglas managed to shut his eyes but not his mouth. He got it full of sand and began gagging.

I let him struggle with it. "But, dead or alive, we've got a problem on our hands now."

"I didn't know what else to do—you understand?"

"You did what you had to do. Now close it up and sit on it before someone else starts nosing around."

Douglas groaned again, rolled over onto his belly and began making motions like a man trying to get up on his hands and knees; but his arms were rubbery, and his legs kept slipping out from under him. It was as if the gravelly sand were strewn with ball bearings.

I rammed a foot between his shoulder blades to ensure that his efforts would be unsuccessful. I didn't want him to get himself oriented before Stringer finished replacing the floorboards overhead. I needn't have worried. Douglas struggled to his knees again, had himself a good barf and then flopped, face down, back into the sand. I stepped aside. Madison cursed. Pretty soon it would begin smelling as foul down in the airway as it did upstairs.

The play of light on the sand at my feet narrowed to the width of a single slat and then disappeared completely. Stringer had fitted the last board into place without further mishap.

In the abrupt return to total darkness, I was again rendered blind. I planted a foot between Douglas's shoulders, not so much to hold him down now as not to lose him in case he should find himself suddenly capable of crawling away. What I really needed was a leash.

I could feel Madison at my side. "What now?" he asked.

"You go back to work on the cinder block. We've got another hour or so down here, and we can't afford to waste it, especially now."

"What do you mean, 'especially now'?"

"I mean that Douglas's arrival here could make confetti of our timetable."

"What's his being here got to do with it? Just tie him up and gag him."

"And what about the roll call?"

"The roll call?"

"Yes, man. The bloody roll call."

He didn't understand, and I didn't have time at the moment to explain it at length. "Just get back to work," I told him. "I'll do what must be done with Douglas, and then I'll join you." I had to deal with Douglas before he regained his equilibrium; otherwise bloody hell might break loose down there in the darkness.

Madison left my side, and there was dead silence for a moment. Suddenly he was back, a brittle note of alarm in his voice. "How the hell am I going to find those same blocks again that we were working on before?"

"Like a blind man. Just keep going until you bump into the wall. Then crawl left as far as you can, with your hand feeling the stone. If you don't find the blocks that have been scooped out, crawl right until you do. They've got to be there."

A long silence was followed by a short expletive as Madison bumped the wall. I knelt and set to work on Douglas. I wanted him thoroughly immobilized.

Rolling him back and forth in the sand to the accompaniment of a symphony of groans, grunts and curses, and finally articulate outrage as his strength returned, I succeeded in stripping him of his shirt and trousers. I tore the shirt into strips.

My first objective was to keep him from crawling off and losing himself in the darkness, and the shirt was the easier of the two articles of clothing to work with. I braided the strips of broadcloth and used them to hobble his ankles. The shirt made an excellent binding, once it was firmly tied—strong enough to prohibit movement, yet of a softness and thickness that wouldn't cut off circulation, as a conventional cord might. Lucky for Douglas. Because if I correctly judged his character, he would make it necessary for us to keep him tied down for some length of time.

I was in the process of tearing Douglas's trouser legs into strips when he began to squirm with alarming vigor. I applied a little extra foot pressure to the broad of his back. If I had to I'd break something to keep him still. No one had invited him to the party.

"In God's name, what's happening?"

"You're being bound hand and foot for the convenience of all, and unless you keep your mouth shut you will be gagged."

"I know your voice!" The officious schoolmarm again.

"I'm told you made a damned nuisance of yourself trying to locate me." I knelt and began working the braided strips of trouser around his wrists. He struggled and tried to wrench his hands free, wriggled into a fetal position, and then rolled and tried to get up

150

onto his knees. "Lie still," I told him. He wouldn't, so I sat down on his shoulders, straddling his back, and resumed work on his wrists.

"Where in God's name are we?" He had turned his face sideways and begun spitting out sand.

"The less you know, the lighter your burden. Now lie still while I finish here, and then I'll help you sit up."

"What? A vestige of humanity? I don't believe it."

"Believe what you like. I believe in economy. I don't believe in waste; otherwise you would never have waked up from the clout on the neck." I tied the knot in the binding on his wrists, rolled him over onto his back and sat him up.

"Is all this restraint necessary?"

"Yes. I try always to do what is necessary. No more, no less."

"Then am I to assume that, not having done away with me, you hope to make some use of me?" He wasn't exactly offering his services.

"Douglas, I have no use for you at all. I should have bashed you and been done with it."

"Why didn't you? Bashing seems to be your line."

"Because you know as well as I do that our jailers make a head count three times a day. I had planned on doing some very necessary work here during the day. If you remain here with me, the head count will come up one man short, unless . . ." I bit off the words. I had said too much, and it was too late to call it back. Douglas was a fatuous ass, but he was quick.

"You say *one* man short. Why not *two* men short? Neither you nor I will be counted." He wasn't aware that Madison was also down there with us, and I wasn't about to enlighten him.

But the damage had been done. There was no shutting him up.

"But you hadn't planned to make roll call at all. You said you planned to stay here, wherever this is, and do whatever work it was that you felt had to be done. How had you planned to get away with that?"

I began to prepare a piece of cloth for a gag.

He hung on like a terrier. "Come to think of it, I don't really recall being aware of your presence on this island until just this morning."

"There are some five hundred people here. You can't know everyone."

"Know everyone? Perhaps not. But one is *aware* of others. I may know fewer than fifty people to speak to, but every thirty days, when the replacements come in, I'm aware of the new faces." He considered this a moment and then blurted accusingly: "*You're* a new arrival. But the last rotation was three weeks ago. You've arrived within the past couple of days. You arrived *after* the island was taken. Who the hell are you, and what are you attempting to do here?"

"Save your precious neck is what. Yours and a few hundred others', before any more blood is spilled." I looped the gag across his mouth. He shook it off violently.

"Do you expect them simply to give us up on demand?"

"Certainly not."

"Then how can you say no more blood will be spilled?"

"No more *innocent* blood. A few of us are prepared to go to some risk to insure that no more hostages will die on this island."

"And our hosts?"

"Hosts?"

"Woden's group."

"What about them?"

"Will their blood be spilled?"

"That will be entirely up to them. It may be necessary."

"Necessary? Only if you and your gang of hoodlums attempt to alter the situation by force. Any action that risks bloodshed is absolutely unnecessary. We have only to wait."

"You're running out of time. Unless something is done in the next forty-eight hours, this island will be awash in blood and oil."

"Then Behzat must negotiate."

"They can't."

"They'll have no choice."

"I'm their choice."

"Then they must reconsider. Surely anything is negotiable."

"Not this."

"But these people want so little."

"They want what is not theirs."

"They have attempted to plead their case by legitimate means. Nobody has listened."

"Maybe they have no legitimate case. It doesn't matter. If you let them win by force what they could not win by reasonable appeal, you have opened the floodgates. Everything gets swept away. That's why I must succeed. And that's why you, unfortunately, are going to spend the next few hours in some discomfort." I dropped the gag across his face again.

"Please!" he begged. "One moment." He had lost his hauteur. I allowed him his moment.

"Perhaps I can help you," he exclaimed. Eager as a deathbed convert.

"I doubt it. I would have made note of your name along with the others if I'd thought you'd be of any use."

"I could make that roll call. The head count would tally up properly. You wouldn't have to take my place. You'd be free to carry on with whatever it is you are doing."

I was sorely tempted. I would have been as relieved to have him out from underfoot as he would have been to go. "And you'd keep silent about everything that's happened tonight?"

"You have my word." Entirely too eager. I couldn't see his face, but I could hear the lie in his voice. I could smell betrayal all over him, smell it above the stink of the rat shit and the vomit. He wanted me to let him go so that he could alert his jailers. Arrogant, self-righteous fool.

As far as he was concerned, the issue was settled. He bent forward to make it easier for me to untie the knot on his wrists. I laid the gag across his mouth and pulled it tight.

He stiffened with outrage. I felt no pity for him. He was an intolerable burden. I would have to make muster in his place. Our timing would be thrown off by hours. Lives might be lost.

I checked the ties on his wrists and ankles and

checked the gag again to make sure he wouldn't choke on it. I hoped he didn't have a head cold which might impair his breathing. He began squirming with considerable vigor. I took that as a sign that he was getting plenty of air. I advised him to settle down and avoid exhausting himself; it would be a long war. Then I crawled off across the tacky sand to find Madison.

We worked side by side, doubling our efforts to do as much as we could before reveille. An hour later we were obliged to quit, but the job wasn't finished. Another hour's work remained to be done. And, thanks to Douglas's intrusion, it would have to be done the following night, when every minute would be critical.

We would have to deal with tomorrow in its own good time. Now it was imperative that we return to the barracks before the other prisoners wakened. We stopped work on the wall and prepared to crawl back to our point of access.

"Lead the way," Madison invited.

I didn't move. I couldn't. I didn't know the way.

The plan had been for us to tap lightly on the loose boards to alert Stringer to the fact that we were ready. If the way was clear, Stringer would remove the boards and help us up. But where in the darkness, in that vast unmarked expanse of flooring overhead, was the spot?

"What's wrong?" Madison asked. He had his fingers hooked around my belt, waiting for me to move out, and I was going nowhere.

"I don't know where it is."

"You didn't mark it?"

"No."

"Shit. We'll be here all day."

He was right. We might spend hours blindly crawling about, randomly tapping the floor if we dared, and alerting half the barracks to our situation in the bargain. I cursed my stupidity. Madison voiced his accord. We were like castaways adrift in the darkness. It was Douglas who tossed us a life ring, though he didn't mean to.

He grunted.

He had heard us scrambling about in the sand, discussing the urgency of getting out, and had become alarmed at the thought of being left alone. He had articulated his protest as best he could—with a grunt—through his gag and had provided us with a beacon to home in on.

How careless to have neglected to mark our exit. How fortuitous to have unknowingly left a marker. Douglas was sitting, bound and gagged, on the spot where he had fallen. He had dropped with plumb-line directness through the opening in the floor. He was sitting now directly beneath our exit. I reached back, tugged on Madison's shirt, and signaled him to follow me.

I tapped the floor overhead, and a moment later the boards began to come away. I checked Douglas's bonds again. In the light from above, I could see that he had reassumed a stoic posture, but his eyes betrayed his anxiety. I understood it; we all share that atavistic terror of the dark.

And then there were the rats.

I advised him to conserve his energy against a time

when he might need it. His penchant for growling and
thrashing about would count for something if the rats
ventured out. We would be back in twelve hours'
time. I could offer him no more than that.

I boosted Madison up through the hole in the floor.
And then, with a hand from Stringer, I hoisted myself
into the dormitory.

# 21

I filled Douglas's place at roll call. Madison made
contact with two prisoners from our barracks whom
he could trust. They agreed to trade places with Jennings and Fletcher after the evening roll call, though
they were not told why it would be necessary.

That evening in the yard, while we ate what passed
for dinner, I sat on the ground with Madison, Stringer,
Jennings and Fletcher and, diagramming in the baked
earth with a finger, laid out our plan of attack.

We would break out of the barracks through the
wall at the rear of the cellar and proceed to the beach
to claim our weapons. Then we would split up into
individual fighting units, each man with a zone to
cover and a specific job to do.

Jennings would be sniper number one and would
situate himself at the edge of the beach, with a sight-
ing angle that would afford him a clean shot at the

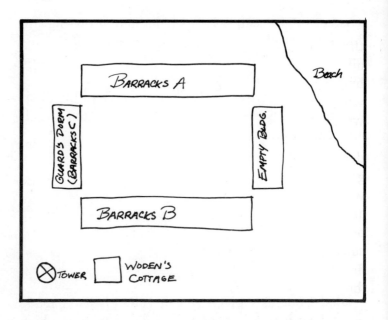

two sentries on the roof of the nearest barracks—barracks A. He would take up this position, clear his weapon for firing, and he would wait.

Fletcher would be sniper number two and would move northward up the beach for about half a mile and then across the high ground of the island in a westerly direction for another half-mile, until he had sight lines for a clean shot at the two men in the airport tower. He would take up this position, clear his weapon for firing, and he would wait.

Madison would arm himself on the beach and then move to a position behind our barracks—barracks A—at the foot of the ladder until one minute before jump-off time. At that moment he would climb the ladder so that he would be at a point just below the lip of the roof when the first shots were fired.

Stringer would move from the beach to a position at the rear north corner of barracks A, out of sight of but almost diagonally across from barracks C, which housed the off-duty occupation forces. His weapon would be cleared for firing, and he, like Madison, would wait.

At that point in time we would have four men deployed and waiting, capable of cutting Woden's gang to ribbons before it knew what hit it. I would work my way a short distance up the beach and around behind Woden's cottage, burst in on him and point out to him the hopelessness of his situation. He could call on his men to surrender before a shot was fired, or he could let them die, and himself along with them.

If he agreed to surrender and ordered his men to lay down their arms and gather in the yard, the day would have been won bloodlessly. If he refused to accept my terms, I would have no option but to shoot him.

In consequence of that act, events would proceed in a prescribed order, but so close upon one another that to all intents and purposes they would appear to be happening simultaneously.

My shot would serve as the signal to attack.

Jennings, sniper A, dug in on the lip of the beach, would kill the two sentries on the roof of the nearest barracks.

The sound of my shots from the cottage to the northwest and of Jennings's fire from the beach to the east should render the two sentries on barracks B momentarily confused. Moments would be all we'd need.

Madison, in his assault position below the lip of the roof of barracks A, would climb the last steps of the ladder. He would expose only his head and shoulders above the roof line. Shooting across the dead bodies of Jennings's targets, he would take out the sentries across the yard atop barracks B with automatic fire.

The sound of gunfire would bring the two lookouts in the airport tower out onto their catwalk, or at least up close to the window glass. In either case, Fletcher, from his sharpshooter's blind, should be able to kill them before they realized what was happening.

Next, with the sentries dead on the roofs of barracks A and B and the yard unguarded, Stringer would be free to move from his position on the north corner of barracks A. He would move through the alleyway to the edge of the yard, where he would have a clear field of fire on the door to barracks C, the guards' dormitory.

Those guards who ran from barracks C into the yard, be they armed or just inquisitive, would be cut down by Stringer. By now Madison would have moved across the roof of barracks A and set himself up in a shooting position on the northwest corner of the roof. From there he could fire down into the windows of barracks C, should any of Woden's men have chosen to remain inside and use their dormitory as a stronghold.

I would have left Woden's cottage and made a dash for the compound. By this time I should be working my way down around the western corner of barracks C, armed with grenades to clean out what pockets of resistance might remain inside.

It should all be over within ten minutes of the commencement of firing. But if I calculated correctly, the first shot would not have to be fired at all. The effect of my confronting Woden, armed with automatic weapons and grenades, should persuade him that surrender was the only logical course open to him and his men.

As I sat in the dusty yard with Madison, Stringer, Jennings and Fletcher and finished laying out my plan, it seemed to all of us that a bloodless transfer of authority was assured.

But I had miscalculated. One oversight in my carefully considered strategy would cost us all dearly.

# 22

That night, when the dormitory was still and the other prisoners had settled into sleep, the five of us lowered ourselves through the opening in the floor for what would be, for better or for worse, the last time.

I reached up and pulled the boards into place over our heads. Then Madison led Stringer, Jennings and Fletcher to the outer wall to finish the work on the cinder block.

I stayed back for a moment to attend to Douglas.

He lay sprawled in the sand just about where we had left him. There was a raw wound on his upper arm, but otherwise he had survived. Maybe the rats had found him indigestible. He had wriggled into a sitting position, and when we dropped down, he began muttering into his gag—obscenities, I presumed—to salute our arrival. A dead rat lay near his ankles. His flailing feet must have broken its neck. It was evident that Douglas had spent some part of the day under siege. I knelt beside him and told him that his ordeal would soon be ended. I had brought a ration of food and water to tide him over. They would be his to enjoy in exchange for a simple affirmative nod of the head to signal that he agreed to behave himself while he ate and drank. He nodded obediently. And this time there was no suggestion of deception. A day in the cellar had wrought wonders.

I removed the gag, and he inhaled noisily and greedily, cursing me between gasps, and then began softly to blubber. It didn't take him long to get himself under control; a stronger character than I had imagined. I tipped some water from a flask into his mouth. He sucked it up thirstily, choked, coughed, cursed me again and asked for more.

I unbound his wrists so that he could finger-feed himself from the cereal box I had brought and could help himself to the rest of the water. I left his ankles tied for the same reason I had tied them the night before: I didn't want to risk his scrambling off in the darkness, up to God knew what kind of mischief, and almost impossible to find.

While he ate and drank I groped my way to the back wall to learn what progress the others were making on the cinder block.

When I returned to Douglas's side, he had emptied the flask of water and finished the cereal. I assured him that the compound would soon be liberated and that he would then be free to go about his business. I rebound his wrists, locking his hands behind his back, and fitted the gag into place. He didn't struggle or protest. Either the long dark day had sapped him of his orneriness, or he sensed that events were coming to a head and that one way or another he would soon be free. My thoughts were on the beach. With four men scraping away at the cinder block diligently and in tandem, the wall was being reduced at a heartening pace.

And then, a piercing whisper. "Devlin!"

I scrambled across the gritty earth, homing in on the sound of the voice as the cry was repeated: "Devlin!" As I got nearer I could hear the men breathing hard with excitement and with the effort expended.

"Devlin!" It was Madison. "We're through."

He placed my hand on the cinder block. It had been scraped so thin that when I exerted pressure with my fingertips, a piece the size of my fist crumbled out as if made of sugar. The cool night breeze found the hole and came whistling through, setting the sweat-soaked laborers shivering. We huddled together as if the battle were already won and congratulated ourselves on our triumph.

I placed a watering eye to the chilly hole and squinted through to see, if I could, whether any of our captors were patroling in the no-man's-land between the barracks and the beach.

Everything was still except for the breeze.

I punched out a little more of the powdery cinder block, cautiously put my face to the hole, and looked both ways. I had a field of view of almost one hundred eighty degrees. There was nothing out there but the sand and the sea and the wall of the barracks around me. I backed away from the hole in the wall, turned to the others, and found myself momentarily blinded by the density of the darkness under the building. I didn't wait to adjust. There was no need to. In a moment we would be out on the beach. "We can go," I said.

I turned back to the wall, raised my foot and kicked out the small section of wall that we had scaled cardboard-thin. It broke away like rock candy.

I took one last look back at where I'd left Douglas. I couldn't see him for the dark. But I could sense his total immobility.

I crawled out through the hole in the wall and flattened out in the sand and waited. Madison wriggled through next, followed by Stringer, Jennings and Fletcher. I got a fix on the spot on the beach a quarter of a mile away where I had buried the equipment, and oriented the others. I estimated it would take in the neighborhood of a minute and a half to cover the distance at a run. I was sure the sentries on the rooftops couldn't see us, but I didn't want us all moving out at once, like a herd; they couldn't see us, but they might sense such a movement and send someone to investigate. We agreed that I would go first, and the others would follow, one at a time, at thirty-second intervals, right in the track of my footprints.

I took a deep breath and broke from the cover of the wall.

# 23

The distance was somewhat greater than I had estimated, and I was breathing hard when I reached the lip of the beach and dove over the embankment into the damp sand. I allowed myself the luxury of ten seconds' rest and three or four deep draughts of sea air before rolling as far away as I could from my landing place. I could feel the vibration through the sand of Madison's footbeats pounding across the nearby embankment. And then a grunt, followed by a full second of nothingness, followed by a thump as he came down smack on his ass almost directly on the spot where I had landed.

"Over here!" I called. And got him moving out of the way before Stringer came sailing over.

One by one we hit that spot: Madison, Stringer, Jennings, Fletcher and I. By the time we were all down on the beach, there was a burgeoning pit, asswide and maybe half a foot deep, where we had all landed.

I found the place where I had buried the equipment and put Madison on watch at the lip of the embankment, while the rest of us dug out my gear and began stripping it of its waterproof wrappings. The good, pungent smell of well-oiled weapons began to mix with the sea air around us.

I was in the process of sorting and dividing up the ammo when Madison set up an alarm. I scrambled across the few yards of beach to the embankment and flopped down at his side.

"Christ!" he whispered. "Look there!" With one hand he was pointing in the direction of the barracks; with the other he was thrusting a pair of binoculars at me.

"Douglas is loose," he said, as I took the night glasses from him and focused them on the back side of the building, where he was pointing. And there to my astonishment stood Douglas, a few yards down from the hole we had punched in the wall, looking this way and that, trying to decide what to do next. His hands were tied and his gag was on, but his feet were absolutely free.

"He came crawling out of the hole in the wall like a worm out of an apple," Madison was saying. "Came out and rolled around on the ground a moment as if he were having trouble righting himself—"

"No wonder. His hands are still tied—"

"Then how in hell did he get his feet loose?"

I knew, but I chose not to say. Overconfidence can kill you. I had untied his hands so that he could eat his dinner, and I had left him to his dinner while I checked the progress of the work on the wall. And in that interval while his hands were free, he must have loosened the bonds at his feet enough so that he could wriggle out of them after we left. I had retied his hands and replaced the gag on his mouth, but I had failed to test the knots around his ankles. Madison and the others had broken through the wall just then and had called me away. But the fault was mine. I had failed to credit Douglas with the proper measure of aggressiveness or resourcefulness.

Now he stood, apparently irresolute, at the rear corner of the building, making squirming movements with his ass to the wall, as if he were trying to scratch his backside on the cinder block.

"Dammit!" I exploded. "The bastard is trying to cut the ties on his wrists."

"Shall I go after him?" Madison asked.

"Too late."

Douglas had freed his hands. I could see blood on his wrists as he brought his hands up to his face to tear off the gag. "Jennings!" I shouted. "Fletcher!" They came running and flattened out in the sand alongside me, their Galils ready. There was a clashing of steel sliding against steel as they cocked their weapons.

I changed my mind. "Forget it."

"Forget what?"

"Douglas is out there behind the building."

"I don't have my sights adjusted yet." Jennings. Cool. Meticulous. Professional.

"Forget it."

Douglas had the gag off and was already moving, stumbling toward the alleyway between the buildings that opened into the floodlit yard. Suddenly his lurching figure stood out in sharp silhouette.

From Fletcher: "Screw the sights. I can knock him down with a burst."

"And let the whole bloody army of them know where we are? Forget it."

Douglas went plunging through the alleyway into the floodlit yard, like a played-out runner at the end of a marathon race. He flung up his hands as if in victory and let out a series of shouts, the sound if not the sense of which carried faintly over the hissing of the gas fires all the way to the beach. Then he stopped and stumbled backward as if someone had struck him across the face. The rattle of automatic fire from one of the rooftops followed a split second later as Douglas pitched back onto the sand and lay still.

"Did they kill him?" Madison asked.

"From the look of it. He's not moving a muscle. But I can't tell for sure."

"Jesus!" Fletcher exclaimed. "From the sound of it, you'd have thought they were shooting at an army."

"Inexperience," I said. "Let's hope they're all that green."

I panned my glasses across the nearest rooftop. One of the young guards there was staring bemused at his weapon, as if it had taken on a life of its own. I guessed that he had done a good deal of the shooting. His partner was gesticulating wildly, as if demanding an explanation.

A moment later the area of the yard that I could see was filling with armed men, looking this way and that for an enemy. They had come spilling out of their off-duty barracks, primed to deal with what must have sounded like an invasion. Maybe some of them were green, but all of them were eager. Another minute and Woden was there, moving in and out among the milling gang, shaping them up, getting them organized. Suddenly he stopped, looked in the direction of the barracks we had fled, and let fly into the air a short

168

burst from his automatic. A warning burst. I could only guess that too many of the prisoners had gotten too close to the barracks windows, trying to see what was going on.

A three-man patrol was dispatched down the alleyway to find out where the bullet-riddled man in the square had come from. It wouldn't take them long. There was no way we could zip shut the hole in the wall in the back of the barracks.

Meanwhile, I could see prisoners pouring out of the barracks into the square. A spontaneous uprising? Not on your life. They were making no aggressive moves toward their captors, and their captors weren't shooting at them. They were being herded out, like cattle. Either there was going to be a mass slaughter, or there was going to be a roll call so that Woden could determine how many more prisoners, if any, in addition to Douglas had got out. Woden was no amateur. In ten minutes' time he'd know that there were four prisoners unaccounted for, and the manhunt would begin.

I had hoped to pin Woden's men down in their positions and force their surrender with a minimum of bloodshed. Douglas, with his well-meant meddling, had blown all of that sky-high. Charging into the square as he had, raising an alarm, he had made inevitable a bloody battle. That he hadn't had time to name the escapees and pinpoint our position can only be attributed to the trigger-happy sentry on the roof. Whether or not Douglas was dead now, I neither knew nor cared. The only thing of importance to me was that whatever his condition, he was unable to speak; otherwise they'd be swarming over us already.

"Jennings. Fletcher. Get those sights adjusted and

load up on ammo. Stringer, get up here with Madison." I slid down off the embankment and finished unpacking our weapons. I passed a couple of Uzis up to Madison and Stringer and set their bags of ammo down beside them. I picked up a Uzi for myself and a bag of ammo and distributed the grenades. There was still no rush in our direction by the armed men in the yard. In fact, surprisingly, the three-man patrol out in back of the barracks hadn't yet discovered our hole in the wall.

I got back up on the embankment again and took the glasses from Madison and watched the patrol and what I could see in the yard. I tried to formulate a scatter plan by means of which we could disperse and chew them up piecemeal. We might manage it. But it would be costly.

One of the three in the search patrol had ambled halfway down toward the beach and was gazing back and forth over our heads, as though whoever had escaped might have tried to swim away. He couldn't see us. But we couldn't move. He'd damn sure see us if we did. So we waited.

The other two on the patrol were foraging back and forth behind the building. They couldn't go on much longer . . . missing the hole or the track we'd made when we beat it for the beach. More carelessness on my part. And, again, because I had underestimated Douglas. It had crossed my mind to send Stringer back to wipe out our trail. But it wouldn't have been necessary if Douglas hadn't raised the alarm. And when it became necessary, it had also become too late.

"Devlin!" It was Jennings.

"Yes?"

"Fletcher and me, we could knock down two of those buggers nosing around the back—maybe all three—before they knew what hit 'em."

"No!"

One of the patrol prowling near the back of the building stopped abruptly, dropped down on one knee and began waving excitedly at the other two. He had found our escape hole.

Jennings, bitterly: "You want us to wait 'til they come after us?"

"We have no choice. The prisoners are still in the yard."

"You think we're going to miss and hit one of the prisoners? If you think we're that shaky, you shouldn't have tapped us in the first place."

"I think if we start shooting now, *they're* going to start shooting. Pure reflex. And the only thing to shoot at is all those people in the yard. So let's not go off half-cocked."

"Shit." That from Fletcher.

Two of the patrol ran back to the yard to tell what they'd found. The third stood with his back to the building and resumed watching the beach. No matter that he didn't know it; he had us pinned down with his eyes.

Minutes stretched out endlessly, like time in a nightmare.

The prisoners began filing back into the barracks. The roll call was over. Now Woden knew how many escapees he had to look for—or thought he knew. He'd be wrong about that, of course, and in my calculations, in the ultimate crunch, his misinformation could be a decisive factor in our favor. There was one more thing that would work to our advantage: he didn't know we were armed.

"Devlin!" It was Madison calling me back to his side. "Jesus, Devlin! Look at them."

I looked, and I didn't need the glasses to see what was happening. The third man on that first patrol, the one who had appeared to be gazing out over the water, must have picked up our trail right off. He had known exactly what he was looking at, even though he couldn't quite see us. Now a dozen or so men— damn near Woden's entire force, except for the sentries on the roof and the pair in the tower—were moving through the alleyway toward the ocean side of the barracks.

When they got clear of the alley they spread out, forming a skirmish line, and began moving toward us across the open expanse of ground between the barracks and the beach.

The closer they came, the wider grew their spacing, as if they were casting a human net which they would ultimately draw shut around us.

Through the alleyway between the buildings, I caught intermittent glimpses of Woden pacing impatiently back and forth as the last of the prisoners filed back into the dorms. I also realized that his force was slightly larger than we had estimated. In addition to the sentries and the men in the skirmish line, there were perhaps half a dozen men in the yard with Woden. In light of what was about to happen, it was a relief to see one of the men in the yard lock the door shut behind the last of the prisoners. They would be safer there than outside.

As for us, we were trapped, thanks to Douglas, with our backs to the water and no place to go except left or right along a narrow strip of sand. We had only two choices. We could throw our weapons into the sea and meekly go back, like lambs to a slaughter—though it wouldn't necessarily be the five of us who would face Woden's firing squad in the morning—or we could dig in and fight.

# 24

They were moving toward us slowly, methodically, but not particularly cautiously. Their weapons were at the ready, but their bodies were not particularly tense. They might have been out for a stroll. They were, after all, rounding up unarmed men. They were well within our sharpshooter's range but still too far off for the rest of us to shoot with maximum effectiveness, and maximum effectiveness was essential. If we were to come through this with any hope of freeing the prisoners, we would have to reduce their force dramatically in the first exchange of fire. After that they would dig in, and in a protracted battle there was no way of gauging what acts of retaliation might be directed against the prisoners. If I let Fletcher and Jennings open up, we'd kill only two of them for certain, and the rest would hit the deck.

The night was cool and there was a breeze blowing in from the sea, but I felt sweat, slippery in my armpits and icy along my back. I wished we could use the waiting time to pick off the two sentries on the nearest roof. It would have been easy shooting for Fletcher and Jennings, and at no cost to ourselves, we would have reduced their number by two. But the sound of firing would have caused the advancing line to dig in just as surely as if we'd been shooting directly at them.

"When, dammit? When?" Jennings anxiously whispered.

"Soon."

I waited until they were seventy-five yards out, within killing range of any of our guns but too far away for them to loft grenades in on us, if they had any to throw.

I could hear them calling to one another. Joking. Relaxed. As if they were on a picnic. An outing to relieve the tedium of their days of routine sentry duty. I wished I could believe that, finding nothing and growing weary of their walk, they would turn back. But they knew we were out there. They had taken roll. And they'd keep coming till they found us.

I staked out a prime and a secondary target for each of us. At this range we might each hit two of them before the whole gang hit the dirt. Battle-seasoned men would dive for cover at the sound of the first burst and then think about where it had come from. I guessed that this lot might do just the opposite.

"At the count of three, fire. One . . . two . . ." We opened up together, like a well-rehearsed orchestra. We dropped our targets, five of them, on the first burst. Two more looked pretty well hit before they all flung themselves down. Almost immediately one man scrambled up and began running in a panic toward the relative safety of the yard. He made about six paces' progress. I don't know which of us brought him down. The others lay flat and began shooting wildly in our general direction.

I could see Woden running down the alleyway toward us. He hadn't the faintest idea what was going on. His first thought must have been that his men had gone berserk and were treating themselves to a turkey shoot at our expense. I saw him. Madison saw him. I yelled to Jennings and Fletcher to draw a careful bead on him and drop him before he was able to absorb what was happening. Stringer saw him, too, and opened up with his Uzi, spraying the alleyway with bullets, to no effect except to save Woden's life. He flattened out against the left wall and then vanished from our sight.

Then everything fell silent.

And then one of the men we had wounded began to scream.

Good. Their dying comrade would do a nice job for their morale.

They opened up again with their assault rifles, to no purpose. Perhaps they were trying to shut out the sound of the screams. Perhaps they were venting their rage.

Silence again. The guns were silent, and so was the wounded man. Perhaps his friends had cut his throat.

I crawled around to Fletcher and Jennings and told them they could sight in now on the two sentries on the nearest roof. The sentries stood atop barracks A in bold silhouette, looking alternately in our direction and down into the yard, apparently oblivious to the vulnerability of their position.

Fletcher and Jennings took their time. Then, *pop-pop*. The silhouettes on the rooftop vanished.

We flattened out in the sand as our two clean shots were answered with another wild fusillade from out front. In the opening exchange we had reduced their force by seven. Then there had been the man who had tried to run back. And now there were the two sentries on the roof. That would be ten out of a force of twenty or so. Not a bad five minutes' work. But we had at least half again as many to kill as we had already killed, and the remainder wouldn't be nearly so easy.

They would have blood in their eyes. And they would know we were armed. And Woden, who was experienced, if few of the others were, would reorganize them along proper lines for hunting down armed men. But he would still not know all the things he should know in order to manage a proper fight. His meticulous roll calls would have betrayed him. He would be hunting four fugitives when he should have been hunting five. And so a plan began to evolve in my mind.

If in a protracted fight our fugitive four could, before they were overrun, reduce Woden's force by half again as many men as they had taken out in the first five minutes of combat, then the fifth unaccounted for and unknown member of our company could, by a hit-and-run tactic, employ his anonymity to devastating advantage.

In other circumstances what I did next might be considered infamous. In the circumstances in which we found ourselves, with not only our lives but hundreds of others' at stake, I did only what was necessary. I abandoned my men.

# 25

I exchanged my Uzi for Jennings's Galil. Like it or not, he would be doing his killing at close range from now on, and he'd have no need for a weapon of special precision.

I put Madison in charge and instructed him to take what toll he could on the advancing force and then to surrender before he was overrun. While they laid down a covering fire, I crawled away up the beach until I had the shelter of the rising escarpment, six feet high on my left. Then I stood up and ran like hell.

The crackle and pop of small-arms fire drifted across the island, a sound like damp kindling burning. It informed me, as I crept up on the airport tower, that Madison and the others—or at least some of the others—were still in fighting shape, still exacting their toll of Woden's men. But enough was enough. Now would be the time for them to quit if they were going to quit at all. Now was the time to lay down their arms and show the white flag; now, while there was still distance between them and the enemy, and while surrender could be considered: before the final rush began from which there could be no turning back. They had done a proper job; now was the time to quit and leave the rest to me.

The two lookouts in the tower had their weapons slung over their shoulders and binoculars up to their eyes, intently watching the fire fight as if it were a soccer match. I had planned to take them out from a distance with the Galil, a chancy business in which I surely would have killed one man outright but probably not the second. But I hadn't anticipated that the fire fight on the beach would continue this long. With the sentries absorbed in what they were watching, I decided to climb the tower and take them at close range, with minimal chance of missing.

The tower was some eighty feet tall, a skeletal steel tower like an oil derrick, open to wind and weather through all its height, except for the enclosed observation deck at the top. This was also steel, a squat cylinder wrapped around with windows and encircled by an open steel catwalk on which the sentries now stood.

I circled north of the tower and came in from behind them, moving quickly into their blind spot at the very base of the tower directly under the observation deck. An iron stairway inside the core of the tower spiraled up the eighty feet or so to the platform where the sentries stood. There was little chance they would see me unless something I did or some sound I made caused them to go to the head of the stairwell and look directly down. Then I would be a sitting duck; my only hope of survival would lie in the steel girders all around, which might deflect enough of their fire to afford me a chance to save myself. But even if in those circumstances I could escape, everything would be lost; I would have lost the advantage of anonymity. Woden would know that a fifth man was loose on the island.

I was halfway up the iron stairway when I heard the thump of the first grenades. Whether my men or Woden's had thrown the grenades, it was the beginning of the end. It meant that the range had closed between the combatants; that the time was fast passing, if it had not already passed, for a safe surrender.

My inclination was to run the rest of the way up the ladder to finish my business on the tower and see what, if anything, I could do to relieve the pressure on my men on the beach. But there were more lives at stake here than just those four.

I checked myself and moved at the pace of a stalking cat. While the two lookouts in the tower couldn't see me climbing toward them, they would have felt my presence had I started to run. The vibration set up by the pounding of my feet on the stairway would have carried right through the steel core of the tower, and they would have felt it in the soles of their feet on the catwalk. One false step, one clang of my weapon against the railing, and it would all be over. So, despite my apprehension about the deteriorating situation on the beach, I crept toward the top.

I came up through the opening in the steel floor of the tower. Through the observation window I could see the two lookouts on the catwalk barely ten feet from me. Their binoculars were trained on the battle. They were totally absorbed in what they were watching.

Any unnecessary movement I made might trigger an alarm. So I stayed where I was, head and shoulders only above the level of the steel floor, like a timorous mole. In a more chivalrous time it might have been considered proper to make some sound, to bring them around, affording them at best a sporting chance, at worst an opportunity to face their executioner. But this was now, and the knights had long ago left the field.

I set my Galil for automatic fire. With one short track of the muzzle, I took off the tops of both their heads. Soundlessly their bodies dropped from sight below the rim of the shattered window. But not before the one on the right, reacting to the sound of the first shots, turned slightly. I caught a glimpse of profile before it vanished. It was the girl, the one who had taken me prisoner and acted as a restraining influence on her hotheaded partner. Too late; the bullets were already on their way.

I bolted up the stairs and out onto the catwalk.

The boy was folded up against the steel bulwark

beneath the window. The girl was gone. It would have been impossible for her to have survived her wound; I had seen her skull shatter. Or had that been the glass?

I pivoted right and left. There was no trace of her. Could she have survived? Could she have crawled around to the other side of the tower? I experienced a brief sense of relief. I had not yet become a killer of women.

And then I remembered that she had a radio with which to alert Woden, and an assault rifle. Reflexively I dropped into a defensive crouch. Would I have to stalk her and do it all over again? Knowing the target, could I squeeze off the shots? Damn! She was costing me time. And there were more lives at stake than hers or mine.

I worked my way around the catwalk and found no trace of her, nor was she making her way down the stairs. But she was gone. I hoped that she had simply run for her life. And I wished her luck. And then, peering down over the railing, straining to see through the Stygian night, I spotted her. On the ground at the foot of the tower. Spread-eagled on the rocky incline. Her body must have slipped under the railing.

Who will remember her grave with roses? Or mine?

I relieved the dead lookout at my feet of his weapon and ammo and his walkie-talkie radio. Then, using the image-intensifying sight of the Galil as a telescope, I tried to size up the situation on the beach.

Judging from the pattern of fire, Woden had reinforced his attack force with the men he had initially held in reserve in the yard. He had spread them wide in an encircling pincers to the left and right of our position. Advancing alternately left, right and center under covering fire from the stationary positions, he had worked his force close in enough to begin lobbing grenades. And the grenades had done their work. It appeared that only two of my men were still employing their weapons; whether the silent two were wounded or dead, I had no way of knowing. But they had done their work well. No more than five of Woden's men were laying down fire. Woden's total force had been reduced to eight: the five on the beach, the two on the roof of the far barracks, and Woden himself.

The automatics were firing relentlessly, but the grenades would do the killing now. Even as I watched, there was a flash to the right of our position on the beach, trailed by the thump of the explosion, and two more of Woden's guns fell silent. Madison, or whoever was still alive down there, had succeeded in cutting Woden's total force to six. Now, now, now, before it's too late, surrender! But why should they? Dammit! By their lights they were winning.

And then, sickeningly, there was another bright flash and a thump on the beach. The grenade must have landed directly behind our position; I could see the airborne spray of water. And the guns fell silent, all of them.

I took the iron stairs two at a time down to the bottom of the tower and ran like hell. I pounded flat out across the crushed lava surface without tacking to find cover or zigzagging to avoid fire. If I had sized up the situation correctly, there would be no one remaining on this side of the island to interfere with my progress. If I was wrong, then everything was lost, because I estimated that I had less than five minutes to set myself down in a position behind barracks B, with its two remaining sentries on top.

The walkie-talkie I had taken from the dead lookout came crackling alive. I pulled up short, dropped to one knee, unstrapped the radio from my belt, and tried to listen. My breath was coming in long, loud gasps: knives in my lungs. The din of the gas fires was as horrendous as ever. The sounds in my body, the sounds in the air made hearing impossible. I flopped over onto my back and pressed the radio tight to my ear and forced myself to take the time to let my breathing return to normal.

Woden was asking for a body count.

So he wasn't on the beach with his men. He had stayed back in the yard and directed the assault from there. The radio went dead. The men on the beach were going about their grisly business. I left the receiver switch on and began to run again in the direction of the barracks.

I took cover behind an outcropping of lava about fifty yards behind the barracks. The two sentries on the roof were silhouetted clearly in the flood of light from the yard. With the sniper sight I could take them out, but the sound of the shots would be heard and Woden would know there was an extra man on the loose, a man he hadn't known existed. He would exercise caution, and that could stymie me and could be fatal to the other prisoners.

The radio began to sputter again.

"How many bodies?"

"Four, at the edge of the water."

"What took you so long? Can't you count to four?"

"It wasn't easy to count. The grenades made a mess."

"And you?"

"We have three remaining."

"Shit."

"Woden?"

"Yes."

"They have hurt us."

"We will hurt them."

"We can't hold so many prisoners with so few of us."

"They are dead men, all of them."

"Woden?"

"Yes?"

"These four on the beach. . . ."

"Yes?"

"Who armed them?"

"My God! They've landed a force!"

There was nothing to be gained by lying low any longer. The advantage of anonymity was gone. I unhooked two of the three grenades I was carrying and set them down before me on the rock. I raised the Galil and took careful aim, twice tracking the sight from the first sentry to the second, timing my move before I shot. The third time, I lined up the sight and fired. The sentries folded up. Then I lobbed the grenades in the direction of the yard. I had no hope of getting close, nor did I care to. God help me if one of the bombs should fall close to a dormitory and maim the prisoners. What I wanted was percussion.

There being no targets of opportunity, I set the Galil on automatic and fired a clip into the air.

"Down on the beach. Down on the beach. Get back here now!" It was Woden shouting into his walkie-talkie.

"We hear them, Woden."

They did think there was a force out there.

"In the tower! In the tower . . ." Woden was yelling for his lookouts in the airport tower. The fire was coming from that side of the island, and he wanted a report. "In the tower. Can you hear me?" His voice was growing strident with anxiety.

I pushed the radio up against my mouth and pressed the transmit button. "Your men in the tower are dead. Surrender. Now. Before it's too late."

"I give you five hundred corpses for my reply."

I unclipped my last grenade and lobbed it, to keep the racket up. Then I slipped out from behind the rock and broke for the yard, the broad back of the nearest barracks shielding me as I ran.

I flattened out against the rear wall of the barracks and fired another clip into the air. Then I slipped along the flank of the building until I came to the alleyway. I rammed in another clip and stole a glance around the corner. The three survivors of the fire fight on the beach were running toward the opposite alley. They had heard the shooting. They were coming to help. Gallant and green as grass. They were nicely bunched as they came into the wash of light from the yard. I rolled out into the alley and came up on my belly flat on the ground fifty yards from them and squeezed off a long burst directly into their middle.

They tumbled forward, carried by their momentum,

wheeling over one another like circus acrobats until they settled into the stillness and the dust at the edge of the square. I rolled back into the shelter of the wall. I still hadn't seen Woden. But he would be more dangerous now than ever. The only question in my mind was, Would he try to kill me first, or the prisoners?

The Galil was empty, and so was my ammunition pack. I flung the useless weapon aside and picked up the AK-47 I had taken from the lookout in the tower.

I slipped along the short sidewall of the barracks through the alleyway until I had the full area of the yard in view.

Woden was running in a crouch, his back to me, crossing the yard from the barracks that had once been occupied by his soldiers to the barracks in which the prisoners were held. His machine pistol was slung over his shoulder. Dangling from his hand, fairly dragging in the dust because of its weight, was a canvas bag. Grenades. He was going to lob them through the windows of the barracks. I could see faces at the windows, gaping in the harsh light. There was going to be a slaughter.

I stepped out from behind the building, pointed my weapon at the small of his back, and squeezed the trigger. Nothing. The damned piece wouldn't fire. The guard in the lookout tower had probably never cleaned it.

Woden was still not aware that I was behind him. He set the canvas bag down on the ground just a few feet below the gaping faces at the window and took out the first grenade. I rushed out into the middle of the square, my useless weapon leveled.

"Halt!" I shouted as if I had an army behind me. "Halt!" As if I had a weapon that could shoot.

Woden whirled, startled. He had already pulled the pin on the grenade; I could see the pin dangling by its ring from the index finger of his left hand. His right hand was curled around the steel-jacketed explosive, thumb on the safety. He needed a moment to assay the situation. I let him take all the time he needed; I really had no choice. I was entirely at his mercy.

But, as far as Woden knew, he was the sole survivor of a misbegotten adventure. I was at the head of an expedition that had all but wiped him out. I was equipped with an AK-47 and was within point-blank firing range. His weapon at hand was an armed grenade. He might try to throw it at me. I might cut him down before he cocked his arm. He could remain immobile and surreptitiously lift his thumb from the safety mechanism and blow himself up. In either case he would be dead. He had better things to do than die. He knew that, captured, he would be treated decently by civilized men. He knew that, given time, another gang would take another group of hostages, and that one of the conditions for the hostages' release would be his release. And so on, endlessly, until those whom he saw as oppressors prostrated themselves through the folly of trying to live by obsolete rules of decorum in a world gone back to the jungle.

Woden carefully fitted the pin back into the grenade, disarming it. He opened his palm and let it drop. It rolled around in the dust at his feet like a malevolent egg, and then it lay still. Woden shrugged resignedly. The war was over—for a while. Let's be friends—for a while. He even managed a smile, disarming me, he thought, as facilely as he had disarmed the grenade. The quintessential confidence artist.

I could see the faces of the prisoners in the barracks—still agape, but the terror gone—looking like children with their noses pressed to a display glass full of wonders.

"Unsling your weapon and set it down at your feet. Touch nothing but the strap."

Woden unshouldered his machine pistol and gingerly laid it down.

"Now step back ten paces."

He shrugged and complied. A regular lamb. I walked to where he had been standing and picked his weapon up. Now I was armed. I was certain that Woden knew how to care for his gun.

I threw away the empty AK-47 I had used to thwart a massacre and trained his own weapon on him instead. His smile faded and his eyes flashed hatred, but only for a moment. He knew he had been tricked, but what was lost was lost. One could recoup tomorrow. He nodded in grudging appreciation and informed me with a look of infuriating arrogance that he considered this reversal of fortune merely temporary.

My finger flexed on the trigger, almost of its own will. The gun bucked. Woden blinked. Five rounds tore through his chest. He staggered back a few steps and then sat down, a look of disbelief on his face. The other side was playing according to a whole new set of rules, and he'd never have time to learn them. He fell over onto his back and lay still, his arms still thrown up over his head in an attitude of surrender.

There would be no hostages taken in his name.

The faces in the window, those same faces that only a moment ago had been agape with wonder at their rescue, now were contorted in dismay, as if I had betrayed instead of saved them.

# 26

I went to the cottage that Woden had made his head-quarters and found the telephone he had used to communicate with the mainland. I called for transports to fly the prisoners out. And medics.

Four of Woden's people were still alive. So was Douglas.

They sent a Lear Jet ahead with a couple of doctors to look after the wounded, and engineers to operate the computers at the control center, just in case the engineers among the prisoners were unable to function.

It was almost dawn by the time they arrived, and two of the wounded were already dead. But not Douglas.

The engineers in the prisoner group had been throwing switches for hours and had shut down the feeder wells all over the Gulf and the holding tanks on the island didn't burst.

The physicians examined the three surviving

wounded and after solemn deliberation and consultation determined that they were still alive. They tapped the veins of their inert clients and began dripping solutions into their systems to tide them over the trip back to the mainland, where they could do a proper job on them with knife, needle and thread.

Two of the three died en route. Douglas lived, and in concert with his wife issued a statement to the press from his hospital bed.

When I arrived in Behzat City late that afternoon on the last transport off the island, I was met by a pair of discreetly pistoled cyphers in plain clothes who escorted me away from the heat and hubbub around the plane.

In a quiet anteroom adjacent to the airport's main reception hall, Minister Hajab was waiting with a handshake, a warm welcome and a "well done." His gratitude was boundless, as was his chagrin.

The domestic situation, exacerbated by Douglas's statements to the press, necessitated my being placed under arrest. Only a temporary measure, I was to understand. Douglas had painted me as a half-mad butcher, and the outlaw Woden had been transformed into a folk hero. An alarming segment of the population was up in arms.

Minister Hajab apologized again for the circumstances that necessitated my detention and assured me again that it would be just a matter of days until it all blew over.

It has been eighty-six days now, and apparently the domestic situation in Behzat remains as rocky as ever.

Not that I have been forgotten by my friends in high places. Hajab is really quite a decent fellow, as much a victim of circumstance as I.

In what is generally a most overcrowded and unpleasant facility, I have a clean, spacious cell to myself and food from the warden's private kitchen. I have books, writing instruments, paper, a comfortable cot and clean linen. I keep myself physically as well as mentally fit. I have all the exercise I want in the yard after all the other prisoners have been marched back inside.

Unquestionably I am a privileged prisoner, but I am a prisoner nonetheless, and the domestic situation shows no sign of stabilizing.

There is a wall out there, and beyond it old comrades-in-arms. The wall is waiting to be breached. My friends are waiting for a sign.

# Afterword

The reader of the foregoing account might conclude that the man who called himself Devlin was successful in his attempt to escape and is again at large. It is my sincerest wish that the evidence could support such a conclusion beyond a doubt.

The escape was to have been effected at nightfall on the tenth day of February. It was never carried out, at least not to Devlin's advantage.

Throughout the first week in February, the domestic unrest which had necessitated Devlin's detention grew steadily worse. On the evening of the ninth the dam broke. The lawful regime was swept away, as were all vestiges of order.

On the morning of the tenth, the prison was emptied of its inmates. Thieves, murderers, dissidents, degenerates—all those incarcerated for whatever cause by the previous government—were designated as political prisoners and were turned loose. Their release was as pragmatic as it was symbolic. Room had to be made for all those who had been affiliated with the previous regime.

There was one exception to the general amnesty on the morning of the tenth. Devlin! He was their bête noir. It was broadcast that he would be publicly tried for his crimes and that a proper penalty would be exacted.

No trial was ever held.

Early in the afternoon of the tenth, a half-dozen of us were packed into the cell he had occupied. Devlin was gone. The only signs of the cell's having been occupied were a small pile of books and papers in a corner behind his cot, and a dark, sticky effluence near the door that could only have been blood. No attempt had been made to tidy things up. It was as if a malignant wind had blown through the room and left only debris in its wake.

We spent the afternoon and early hours of the evening unattended and unfed. Tapwater was plentiful from the sink in the cell, but I am certain that had our captors been aware of this small source of comfort, the water would have been turned off. But they were occupied with other matters. There was sporadic shooting all over the building. At random? By design? Who knows? We prepared ourselves for the worst.

As night fell, the building grew quiet. Perhaps the animals were sated. Perhaps they were merely exhausted. I began reading the papers that Devlin had left behind. When the sun set, I could read no more. Our captors had failed to turn on the light in the cell. Perhaps they had forgotten us. Or so we prayed.

I began to doze in the corner where I sat, the envelope containing Devlin's papers in my lap.

Suddenly the night erupted. The cell door was blown off its hinges. A man armed with a submachine gun waved us out. We fled before him down the dark, smoky corridor. Two armed men bracketed the doorway at the head of the exit tunnel. A dead guard lay at their feet.

"Where's Devlin?" one of them asked.

I told them about the empty cell and the blood. They exchanged quick looks. No more words were spoken. The leader made a sign to leave.

They neither ordered us to follow them nor did they make any effort to stop us. Their goal now was escape. If we escaped with them, they had no objection.

Another dead guard lay at the end of the exit tunnel, watched over by another of Devlin's armed friends.

And then we were free. A Land Rover was waiting. The four raiders sped away.

We scattered.

I lost myself in the dark, chaotic streets and came at last to a haven. I realized then that I was still carrying Devlin's papers.

I hid and preserved the papers for the most base of reasons: if captured, I might be able to trade them for my freedom.

I made my way across the border, planning to return when order was restored. So much for plans.

I live as best I can, forever a guest in foreign lands, bartering what I can to live: a nomad, in my way, like my fathers before me. So much for progress.

Devlin's body was never found.

A prisoner who had occupied the cell across from his on that frenzied morning recalls seeing Devlin's cell entered by an armed rebel and hearing the rattle of automatic fire within. After a lapse of minutes, an armed man backed out, dragging a corpse, and then vanished from sight. Whether the man who entered the cell was the man who left it, the prisoner from across the corridor could not say.

Whoever it was who left the cell on that bloody morning, Devlin is no more. He was only the most recent of countless incarnations. He shed his name and identity as a snake sheds its skin.

Four hundred ninety-eight captives on the island of Dhasai owe their lives to him, as I owe mine. How many others are in his debt, I will not venture to guess. Of the man who called himself Devlin, this account is all that remains.

A. M. Hajab

Former Minister of Interior
Former Kingdom of Behzat